playing

in the

asphalt

garden

jill battson
phlip arima
stan rogal
t a t i a n a
freire-lizama

insomniac press

Editor: Mike O'Connor

Copy editors:
Lloyd Davis
Zaf Gousopoulos
Waheeda Harris
Dave Waldner

Canadian Cataloguing in Publication Data

Main entry under title

Playing the asphalt garden

ISBN 1-895837-20-0

1. Canadian poetry (English) - 20th century.*
2. Short stories, Canadian (English).* 3. Canadian
fiction (English) - 20th century.* I. O'Connor,
Mike, 1968-   .

PS8279.P53 1994   C811'.5408   C94-931715-2
PR9195.25.P53 1994

A number of Jill Battson's poems were first published in the
following publications: *Endangered List* in *Contemporary Verse 2*, *In
Summer* in *The Muse*, *Netsuke* and *Circus* in *Acta Victoriana*, *Nicked* and
The Hanging in *Venice West Review*, *Strand +* in *Frogmore Papers*. Stan
Rogal's short story, *Freckles*, was first published in Quarry Magazine.
Tatiana Freire-Lizama's poem, *The Mountains Back Home*, was first
published in Quarry Magazine.

Printed and bound in Canada

Insomniac Press
378 Delaware Ave.
Toronto, Ontario, Canada
M6H 2T8

editor's note

Playing in the asphalt garden is an analogy of urban writing. It captures the contradictions of life in the city — between rich and poor, powerful and powerless, new and old. It also speaks of creativity in a place that has been built, as opposed to having grown.

It is not the city of buildings and streets, but an environment where the writer creates and is influenced by the composite of human experience. The city is a concentration of human experience; where a rapid and voluminous exchange of ideas, messages, power and beliefs takes place. It is the city as the landscape of the human mind.

The reader can sense the city looming around each writer as they create their stories, even if the story doesn't take place in a city. The pervasive influence of the urban context is a constant companion to each piece.

These writers express the urban experience from the multiplicity of addiction and grittiness of the street to the complexity of control, identity and desire in relationships to the sense of longing and pride of immigrants looking back at where they came from.

In this garden one can feel the energy, hear the sounds and dream the dreams of the city.

— *Mike O'Connor*

THE ENDANGERED LIST
THE ENDANGERED LIST
THE ENDANGERED LIST
THE ENDANGERED LIST
THE ENDANGERED LIST

written by Jill Battson • designed by Shilling Chau

CIRCUS

Sometimes I am a circus
and you are my fat lady
awash with Melville's legend
and the sweat of a thousand
sexual encounters with
sideshow freaks and red dwarfs
that whoop and carouse inside me
when I travel long distances
in my car that has no radio

Fat lady, you are my double Adonis
twice wider and deeper
than I want to be
sitting outside my trailer
you loll peeling grapes
on an upturned orange crate
groaning under your weight
while I secretly thumb
through inky personals
looking to replace you
with a bearded lady
a tattooed lady
in my room stark and neat
books alphabetically filed
bedding hidden behind
fake wood panelling
on which a postcard of
Leonardo's Cartoon is tacked
perfectly symmetrical
to the grooves in the pressed sawdust

my billet immaculate
as yours is Dionysian
empty wine bottles strewn
suspended eternal
leaves of typewriter paper
concertina solidly in air
heavy with the aroma of
fermenting fruit
warmed by candles
of sculpted grease and glass
kitchen knife twangs
in the wall
next to a dishevelled bed
heavily indented with your form

I heave when I am there
smothered by chaos

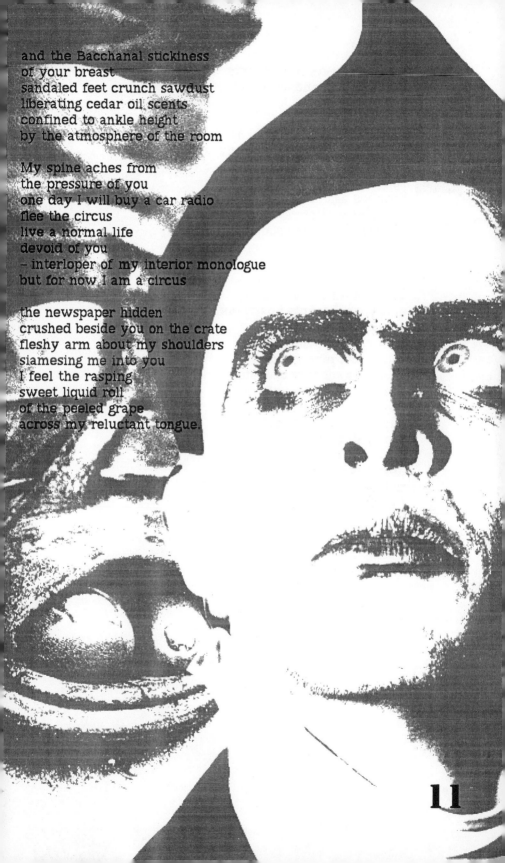

and the Bacchanal stickiness
of your breast
sandaled feet crunch sawdust
liberating cedar oil scents
confined to ankle height
by the atmosphere of the room

My spine aches from
the pressure of you
one day I will buy a car radio
flee the circus
live a normal life
devoid of you
– interloper of my interior monologue
but for now I am a circus

the newspaper hidden
crushed beside you on the crate
fleshy arm about my shoulders
siamesing me into you
I feel the rasping
sweet liquid roll
of the peeled grape
across my reluctant tongue.

11

S.
those beautiful Italian suits
and your philandering ways
behind my smile
the gold ring
lay on the back of my tongue
threatened to slide down my throat
an oft-used fellated gesture
spat out of my mouth
bounced against the plaster of the wall
still a perfect circle
but the sound, the sound
it is marriage.

M.
that beautiful body
and your disappearing ways
we danced in the dark
on a rain-drenched deck
rough soft pine under
unctuous subtlety of water
rain rivulets blue with moon
twist down my breasts
hand over your bicep
the lightest touch
it is hard and full
desirous fingertips
the lies come out of your mouth
like projectile vomiting
but the sound, the sound
it is melody

You extend masterfully over me
thread the needle
watch while I sleep
static diamond of an eye fizzles
blinking reflections of pornography for bisexuals
there is a point of light
that illuminates the tissue-ality of
undernourished flesh
there were oranges
there were pekoes
and there was you
spongy soft
silk-screened gold sepia
the light always comes from the left.

STRANDS+

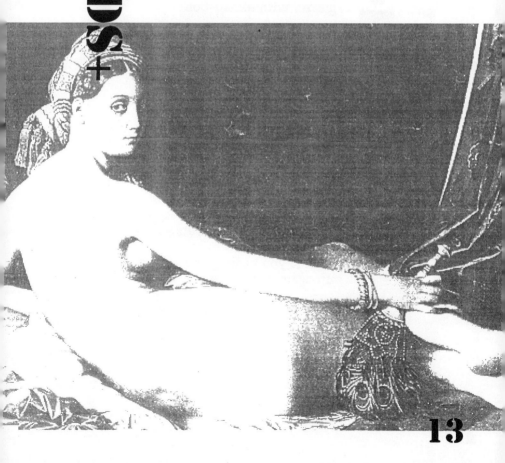

13

I watch the progression
beat sideburns lose definition
I want to cut into the hairs of your face
carve my designs with a cut-throat razor
stubble titian and cable like
unique story of cellular life in high gloss
growing towards promise

carve you in the soundless room
cautious yet stuffily hysterical
window slits through which light cannot escape
spores of mould spread above plexiglas
the piano speaks chopsticks
I have tribal ideas
you are solid and warmly damp
glisten with exhaustion

there is just one obsession here
and you are it
sharpening the razor
I tell sexual dream tales
promise Harvey H and Henry M
(sans Paris)
tighten down with Mitzvah technique
half serious and it shows

I want to feel the sound of you in my throat
until my body
releases
the gilded box of secrets
within my chest
I want you bearing my marks
up against the smeared mirror of my heart

shaving is just the beginning.

P FOR A

NETSUKE

I hang from the waist
of a man I've never seen
counterbalancing bags of tobacco
handfuls of coin
revolving anticlockwise
bumping and uncontrolled
when we walk
I see flashes of people
hurrying on the street
then cotton material
then people again blurring by
streaks of colour and black
my ungiving surface
flesh cold and hard
touches no one
warmth from his body
whispers to the surface
of the fabric which
remains cool against my skin
as we sit at tea
faces frozen gnarled and grizzly
my hands clutch at a cane
that keeps me upright
dowager hump pressing
through body
to palms holding fast
when he dies
I will pass to a geisha
I long to dangle from her waist
silken rope gliding the length
of my body
through anus to skull
cheek pressing on perfumed silk
as she dances slowly with me
warmed by steaming water
and the softness of her hands
breathing life into my body
still for so many years
I would hasten his death
drop poison into his food
if I were not fashioned from ivory
bound by leather

15

IODINE (for vic)

She slapped me
domino crack of the bamboo whisk
and all I could think of
was 173 partially burned fetuses
smouldering under the high Oklahoma sky
sucked from 173 wombs
as she held out the snake bite kit
and told me she thought
large nipples were beautiful

With macro vision I looked past
Chippewa eyes
almond and chocolatey dense
to the single liver-length braid
bound with the hide of a negro
hovering above a muscle tensed spine
backed up to a window
steamed with passion
my initials next to a fist
through the transparent 'J'
I could see the late-night street
two floors down
a black man waxed his burgundy cadillac
in the cool
the whiteness of his terry bathrobe
bled into the soot of his skin

He gave me the thumbs up
to remember a man I loved once
who now seems so ancestral
he waxed his car with the fat of the poor
and beat me red to purple to ochre
when I refused to be gagged

Awoken from visions
by the soft heat path of
her leather-gloved hand
rough seams over the fingertips
scratched the rim of my navel
manifesting her strength
into the left hand behind my head
she dragged down the knotted muscle
that was my neck
and whispered in my ear
'I am the lesbian who beat
my tiny baby to death'
and I felt the rush of an iodine injection
through the girdle of my pelvis.

IN SUMMER

You left a bowl of fruit
on your kitchen table
ripening
rotting
with imperceptible movement
splitting open with its mushy
overpowering sweet odour
of neglected summer
seeds and stones struggling for earth

You lay on the white hospital bed
ripening
rotting
the fruit of your body
unable to burst open
moulds
in fluid containment
white yeast
visible in your mouth when you speak
invisible in your esophagus, vagina
it is the summer of your life

I remember photographs
in restaurant windows
as we walked on the Danforth last year
anglo-greek dishes
'gyros', 'donar kebabs'
pita bread wrapping its labia caress
around olive
tomato
folds of sliced meat
and tzatziki
white, yeasty fluid
yoghurty and thick
coating everything
and I remember laughter.

17

Mother, read the news to me
as I sip warmed milk
comfort food of my childhood
I am unable to eat a
boiled egg without my parents
should I crack or slice
a chicken's bloodied mess
congeals yellow on my spoon
buttered soldiers stand to attention
did I mention my uncle
sits in the house of lords?

when I was a child star
I tap-danced my way
across the airwaves
became a zombie in x-rated b movies
directed by my grandfather
his metal megaphone
boomed in the ears of studio bosses
star material, star material

my image beams through black space
satellite crisscrossed miles
to tease the viewer's eye
with a pinpoint of light
complete my face with persistence of vision
on my brother's television network
he fills the screen
tells the public
watch her, watch her

Father, guide my pen as I write
sweat over a bad novel
too long
time-confused colloquialisms
he runs his fingers along
the spines of self-penned books
editions in leather, in French
behind the back of his hand
he insinuates into the ears of the publisher
New York Times bestseller, New York Times
bestseller

THE FAMILY FIRM

18

My mother's voice sings on CD
valium heavy
slurred with fear
a reminder of drug abuse
the death certificate read
accidental death
congratulations

Mother, sing to me
read me the news and the famous five
I'll sip my milk
managed to eat the egg
choked down a bereaved throat
worry about focus and ruin
mired in this much nepotism
my mediocrity can only succeed

19

MY FATHER'S DAUGHTER

Out of red tee shirt sleeves
her arms hang
midsummer tan
wrist-bone tight and gleaming
there is everything fabulous
about the back of a body

      she walks away from me

dust wafts from the path
escapes the sides of unlaced sneakers
billowing from ninety pounds
four o'clock dead heat
threatened by electricity
of storm meets humidity
meets meteor shower

      she walks away from me

sneakers damp inside and
farting in the gap of arch
pale straight hardness
of Achilles tendon
unsocked ankles
are my favourite part
sultry day feels as if
there will never be a wind again

      she walks away from me

curved neck
satin highlight of muscled spine
disappearing under
sun shaft frizz of curly hair
smooth bark
to the canopy of foliage
I am a tree hugger

      she walks away from me

my skull packed with storm migraine
heat and dust
neck and ankles
they come from me
they belong to me
I have felt her body
for the last time

      and she is walking away from me.

She is weathered by the sun like the grey
plank siding
of their Long Island mansion
paint carelessly splashed on the screen door
white and peeling
nothing but promise
she could have done anything
married anyone
when she lived on Park Avenue
millionaires were always asking
faded aristocracy in faded elegance
now she's just plain crazy
came back from New York City in 1952
to care for the mother she loves
mother she hates
mother and lethargy enslaved her

GREY GARDENS

Sea of green, sea of leaves
below the balcony
drop a favourite blue silk scarf
and never recover it
could have married Eugene
but mother sent him away
he asked her
how someone so warm on the telephone
could be so cold in person
and that was the end of Eugene
too young for her anyway
salt humid breeze
coming in from the sea peaking
summer turquoise between boughs

Cats run around with eight toes each paw
humbug striped
looking kind of coonish
she was so beautiful at twenty
in the portrait propped cockeyed on the floor
cat squats behind it
and she laughs
lays the New York Times on her bed
so another cat can shit there
amidst empty ice cream containers
and decapitated flowers

The grocery delivery boy comes
and the gardener comes
and some guy called Lenny
in a baseball cap comes

21

and the Times comes
and somehow everyone gets paid
she feeds her mother
corn on the cob and iced birthday cake
martinis in mason jars
and they sing
– only a rose I bring you

She waltzes through the hall
black lace scarf
underneath the bodice of her swimsuit
makeup heavy from the sixties
ribbons wound round ankles
white shoes
waltzes to loud military marches
on the record player
waving an American flag
into the dining room and back
accompanied by mother yelling
Edie
from the bedroom above where cats shit
and corn boils on a hot plate
tea for two
duelling gramophones
duelling mother and daughter
and that's the way it's going to be 'till somebody dies.

22

THE ENDANGERED LIST

My table on the African reserve
roughly hewn wood
split and held
by oxidized nails
I am desperate for civilization
        civilization is sunglasses
the cheetah leapt
soundlessly onto the table
hovercraft feel of
        living leather pads
        popcorn smell
        smell of parched plains
laps from my
cereal bowl
today is cocoa puffs
coarse stickiness
endangered fur rasping under my nails
        coat would look good on me
        waiting at Grand Central in my
        sealskin go-go boots
rifle beside table
        propped
        loaded
        cocked
one shot is all it takes

at this precise moment
somewhere in the alps
bordering Italy
        in baggy black goretex
        leopard print sweater
        borrowed sunglasses
the endangered species:
the Pope skis

23

CONFESSIONS OF

posing the way I used to when I thought people noticed
they are opium-crazed, outline of beautiful shoulders blur into fog
dampness mingles with smoke
and all is pressed down by black looks and gravity
concrete around the pool pulsates
veined with cracks that draw mist inside
dragon's breath
three dragons with breath that coils up out of cracks and down

I will write soon

The pipe, tarnished silver, ornate with swirls of filigreed metal
rests cool on my swollen bottom lip
the bowl, hot and conductive in the well of my palm
sucks opium and air
there is nothing save the accelerated explosion of heartbeat
so heavy in my head as if my body's ten pints of blood
have sucked up into my brain
the sound accompanies rattling crescendo of rain
one drop will soak a full-grown man
fashion models race dragons for shelter
and I am desperate for anyone to speak, break the illusion
that I am the only writer, the only poet on the Peak.

AN OPIUM EATER
-THE POEM

Darkness has scuttled in like so many hot goblins licking at ankles
tornadoes of mist swirl in slow motion around the house
typhoon season

tonight I must write

sweat so concentrated, the very tips of my fingers stick to keys

it is piano
it is typewriter

it is absorbed by the light-smeared kaleidoscope of condensated windows
house looks out over the harbour
I am in the place of the Governor
received a transfusion of Noel Coward's blood – and it was tainted
nothing

then after three weeks
the urge to write in a dressing gown and bow tie
up here, I am sequestered from the languid crush of fashion models
who pack the bars of the Roppongi
a displaced few lounge by my pool wearing sunglasses in the dark

What is it like to
hang from the neck
until dead?

THE HANGING

Ask Ruth
last woman
her beautiful white neck
sculpted from water and alabaster
held softly in the hand of the hangman
who will tighten the rope
pull the lever
drop her three feet
dangling
paying for the crime of passion
her unfaithful man
many times over

Ask Albert
career hangman for 25 years
like his father before him
the rough and smooth throats
of 450 men and women
once in 24 hours
27 war criminals
graced his gallows
swinging in the drizzle
of a grey october day

Ask me
the asphyxiation
each time you meet
that woman
that boy
in dark alleys
of swirling dampness
trousers soaked to your knees
stinking of sweat and blood
musky sex smell
an invisible aura around you
silk stocking
leather thong
hanging from your hand
like a garrote

Ask me
how it feels
to hang from the neck
until dead

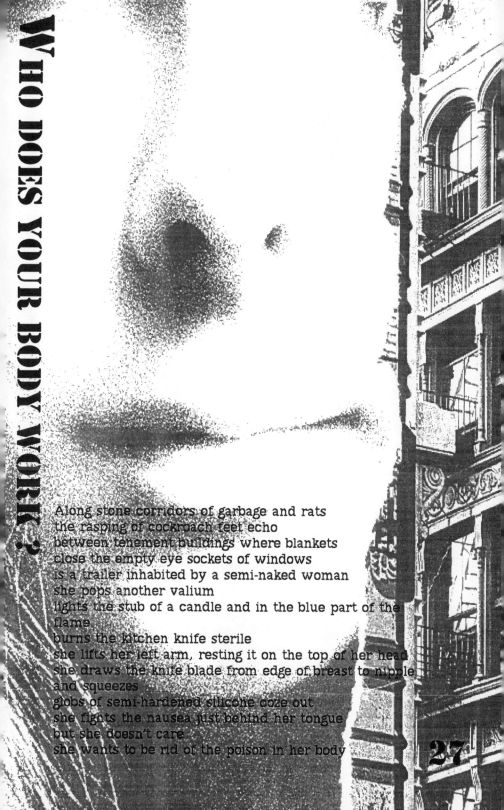

WHO DOES YOUR BODY WORK?

Along stone corridors of garbage and rats
the rasping of cockroach feet echo
between tenement buildings where blankets
close the empty eye sockets of windows
is a trailer inhabited by a semi-naked woman
she pops another valium
lights the stub of a candle and in the blue part of the
flame
burns the kitchen knife sterile
she lifts her left arm, resting it on the top of her head
she draws the knife blade from edge of breast to nipple
and squeezes
globs of semi-hardened silicone ooze out
she fights the nausea just behind her tongue
but she doesn't care
she wants to be rid of the poison in her body

27

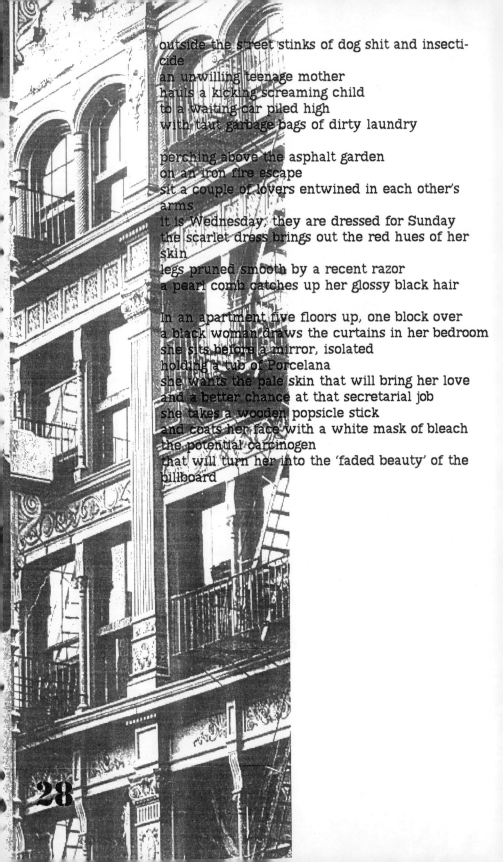

outside the street stinks of dog shit and insecti-
cide
an unwilling teenage mother
hauls a kicking screaming child
to a waiting car piled high
with taut garbage bags of dirty laundry

perching above the asphalt garden
on an iron fire escape
sit a couple of lovers entwined in each other's
arms
it is Wednesday, they are dressed for Sunday
the scarlet dress brings out the red hues of her
skin
legs pruned smooth by a recent razor
a pearl comb catches up her glossy black hair

in an apartment five floors up, one block over
a black woman draws the curtains in her bedroom
she sits before a mirror, isolated
holding a tub of Porcelana
she wants the pale skin that will bring her love
and a better chance at that secretarial job
she takes a wooden popsicle stick
and coats her face with a white mask of bleach
the potential carcinogen
that will turn her into the 'faded beauty' of the
billboard

BUDDY CAN...

United States Marine Corps served in Vietnam — he began his litany of why we should give him our spare change that morning I rode the New York subway downtown. Belting under the exploded World Trade Centre heading for Bleeker. Bowery Derelicts Fear Poverty. The Lexington line is a world where blacks aggressively campaign for cash. Fight Bicker Kill. Perhaps you. The 21st century is already here. He closes in with his Kentucky Fried Chicken breath, his KFC soft drink cup jingling. Eyes swollen. Skin shiny from the alcohol we have provided. It is the dead of winter. The coldest day in New York history. The subway car is sub-zero yet he lifts his shirt, twirls like a runway model to show the shrapnel scars on his side and back. Inchlong raised slivers eerily regular. The colour of scrotum skin. He rolls up his sleeves. Patches of wine-coloured AIDS-related Kaposi's Sarcoma cover his arms. He says it's a cancer caused by agent orange. We are only animals. Passengers unconsciously look death in the face. Shut down. Dementia gives good timing. He leaves the car at the next stop. Bleeker. Patrons. Easy Marks. Suckers. Forgotten as he counts his change. How much medicare can a homeless person buy?

THE GRIP OF ELVIS

Confused by rain
warmed by the road
the bird lingered
hopping slowly across the lanes
to become a statistic
in my road-kill journal
smacking into my reluctant radiator
at 50 miles an hour
dying among squadrons of butterflies
kamikazed over the days
guilt eternal and amplified

you were huddled with Elvis
grinning behind motorized sunglasses
about the time I crossed into South
Dakota
cattle standing diagonal to the road
rumps defending faces
resigned stupidity on chewing jaws
beaten by hail
the size of large rhinestones

sheets of storm
gathered across the plains
before fissure of mountains
soft whirlpool of mercury
revolving, enfolding the Black Hills
Crazy Horse looking out
the same way for twenty years
small plants defacing the whiteness
of hewn granite
pointing
in the direction of the hail
the herd
the white boy
running in the sulphur twilight
blond hair shrieking
neo-Aryan neo-Aryan
pointed urgency through my pulse
quickly halfway across America
to reach you
pull you from coloured emulsion
save you from the grip of Elvis
your one hand clutching white leather
the other a cormorant
blue-black feathers embossed
with the shape of a radiator grill

CHILD IN THE GROCERY STORE

In the grocery store I jangled my cart
with the obstinate wheels
up and down the violet
of fluorescent aisles
smell of the charnel house
delicately in the air
portuguese widows
black spiders
stealing handfuls of grapes
jamming them into their mouths
blue-red spittle dribbling
language –
their excuse for ignoring the signs

I heard sobbing
and there under shelves of canned beans
crouched a toddler
bald and wailing
squeezing crocodile tears

reaching down to comfort him
the open mouth shot into a sneer
exposing two rows of jagged teeth
he grabbed to pull me under
into his sulphurous baked bean lair

I stumbled back against the cart
losing my balance
falling sideways
hard onto the linoleum
propelling myself backwards
across the cold floor
scuttling
the child laughing
darting its tongue
through sharp teeth

I backed onto
warm stockinged legs
looked up
to a circle of black-clad women
all purple spittle and hard-eyed grins
reaching down for me.

with the shape of a radiator grill

The tartness prickling my tongue
I spit the hard-boiled lump of sugar candy
onto the pavement
where it shatters into a hundred

saliva-glistening pieces
shrapneling out in many directions

NICKED

as I look up to see the shards
of green-blue reinforced glass
hanging out of the side of my car
where the back window used to be
Welcome to L.A.
is what my landlord said
when I complained the security parking
was really
false sense of security parking

now I can't keep my eyes off
the jumble of blue, green, red wires
spewing out of the dash
twisted together with black electrical tape

dangling with loss
and I think of you

32

crouched over your mother's toilet
open-mouthed in silent anguish
but afraid to make a sound
as you dropped the baby
from your womb
slipping on broken waters
over white porcelain
to be swathed in a towel
and hidden in a drawer
until the family cat discovers it
two weeks later
decomposing

the wires wave at me
begging to be put back
to be connected to their placenta radio
so they can throb again with the heartbeat
of music

when I look up to the
traffic jam eternity
that is the Hollywood Freeway
I see a dirt-covered
pink plastic dildo
all rippling veins
abandoned, but hopeful
standing to attention
at the side of the road

33

THE GREY

The gate snaps back
the horses leap away
shooting out onto red earth
sponging under metalled hooves

Always bet on the grey horse
my Grandfather told me
when I was nine and sweaty-handed
mine enclosed in his work-scarred one
we watched them jump Beecher's Brook
on a grey drizzle day at Epsom

At Santa Anita, many years after my Grandfather's death
my racing form leeches ink
onto the sweat-covered palm
that crushes it in a tight fist
as I watch the grey gallop away
from the gate
terracotta earth misting
the dappled legs
I'm alone in the cheap seats
packed in with Hispanic farmers
in their smooth grey stetsons
and white patent leather shoes
they are whipped into a frenzy
by the commentator
whose echoing voice accelerates

34

in the second half mile
taking my heart with him

a voice in the back
calls the name of a horse
the name of a jockey
the name of a deity
and my grey horse
is beaten by the jockey
sweat erupts from her flank
as the crop smacks home again

The crowd on its feet, frantic
I am rigid with the excitement
of the sport of kings
my horse crosses the finish line
first, last, third
and my Grandfather says
'Bet on the grey'

I look down to my hand
fingers unwrap the damp ticket
that just bought lunch,
entrance, gas, rent
and I'm very near
the rim of crying

It was my fault entirely
I wanted to be allowed
through the gates of heaven
shake the warm hand
of St. Peter in both of mine

I studied the holy scriptures
in spare moments
and coffee breaks
at my part-time job

I adhered the fish
to the back of my Malibu
when at last I became
a born-again Christian

only trouble was
I inhaled too many
regular, regular plus
super plus and diesel fumes

I got birth defects
from being born again
at Dirk's Discount Gas Bar

BORN AGAIN

THE QUEEN MARY

Cosmetics blur into reality
in lights as dim
as the underneath of a midnight bridge
along the rive gauche
I am the only woman with real breasts
around me shriek the hags of transformation
pickup lines I have never heard

I like your seams

the girls tower above me
barrels of body in tart clothes
the occasional librarian
clings to the wall
ultra-polite men unusually handsome
treat the women with deference
a tenderness reserved for treasured love
eyes loiter
at every round buttock
stressed cleavage
asian face
black leg
exotica
their shapes cantilevered
over barely worn shoes
heels at any height are hard to walk in
I see the tension in the way they dance
the male gaze personified
hair and hair and hair
caterpillars resting on eyelids
artificial slash of red
curved as talons in the blue air
these are the men who transvest themselves
paradoxical
hormones versus silicone
the amputated penis
will I pass in this light
for once, I am not the only one
wondering if I look attractive
I am a woman
under mild duress

37

crowded
rooms
subway
platforms

written by phlip arima

designed by mike o'connor

Rain

in my mind

are large black clouds

obscuring memories

from age ten on down

on down to when

i wasn't

walking down this street

seeing a child

who doesn't see me

in his haste

running as if late

for something i don't know

something important at that age

something i wonder if he'll remember

a moment later

it is beginning to rain

water washing down

masking all sound

of a once sunny summer day

and i think to myself

as the boy is long gone

that clouds will always

eventually rain.

A Dance For Auntie

rent the box, leave me nude,
lay me out with eyes stitched wide.
please comply with this request.

i am dancing on a boardwalk of rotting wood. the tide is in.
a gale force storm watch has been announced. my
fingernails need sanding. my jeans a new zipper. my teeth
replacement.

auntie use to say: rock 'n rollers who we believe o.d.'ed are
on extended tours managed by aliens from another galaxy.
she also held that Elvis is dead. she fell off an eight storey
roof after taking too much speed.

i am pirouetting around a post where the railing is broken.
an imagistic waltz for the gulls to watch. my lover has no
feet for me to clumsily step on. the wind creates white caps,
bites at my face.

let the sulphur burn away before you suck in the flame. let
the cigarette dangle at the corner of your mouth, not stick
straight out from your face. always inhale as much as you
can. i'll know when you're faking 'cause the smoke won't
blow straight.

auntie never taught me how to make rings.

Slow Burn

It is a persuasive madness
       lurid like an autumn wind
              at three a.m.

when teenage boys in dark denim (testosterone humping
up their systems) gather to saunter streets and alleys
searching for the key to stay sultry cool,

when unemployed, bulging eyed BBSers fixate on their
fuzzy screens hoping to discover some downloadable data
detailing the purpose of existence or, at least, some new
joy-stick fun,

when insomniac home-makers weep in front of their
televisions as credits for films they once watched on high-
school dates float to a score no radio station plays
anymore,

when gas-bar attendants nod off and doberman guard-dogs
yawn and the booze-cans along the fringe of every trendy
zone swell with bodies too hyped or too lonely to go home
to bed,

when donut shops, bus shelters, doorways and public
parks become the bedrooms of the homeless; and
newspaper presses finish printing the daily statistics,

42 crowded rooms subway platforms

when 976 operators, begging for water, bite their chapped
lips and strippers wash their sweat-streaked skin and pimps
start bitching and cops stop caring while so many people
still manage to sleep,

                                   a madness

without energy for anger,

                                   a madness

the diversion manufacturers
and lottery machine use – abuse,

                                   a madness

bearing activist and reformist
from the same womb,

                                   a madness

whose stink rises
like an increasing chronic pain
that doesn't seem so insidiously horrid
until a gentle touch makes it all too apparent.

                           It is a persuasive madness.

In The Sun (a song)

twenty-one children in the sun playing with their guns.
twenty-one children in the sun, i'm the tallest one.

listen to the state when it tells me how to stand straight.
listen to the tv when it tells me how to wash my face.
the diet that i eat is sanctioned politically correct.
the drugs i abuse i purchase with a doctor's consent.

i don't wear leather. i don't wear fur.
i don't use products tested on laboratory pets.

twenty-one children in the sun standing for the national anthem.
twenty-one children in the sun, i'm the best one.

salute the desert storm, salute the arms race.
salute exploration into outer space.
trust star wars implementation
will let us rule the peace.

i canvas for trees. i canvas for seals.
i canvas for the things i'm told are fashionable.

twenty-one children in the sun marching to the media drum.
twenty-one children in the sun, i'm the goose-stepping one.

nothing that i buy endorses pesticides.
nothing that i buy destroys the ozone layer.
i walk and i bicycle and i won't ride in cars
and given the choice i wouldn't move at all.

twenty-one children in the sun playing with their guns.
twenty-one children in the sun, i'm the best one.

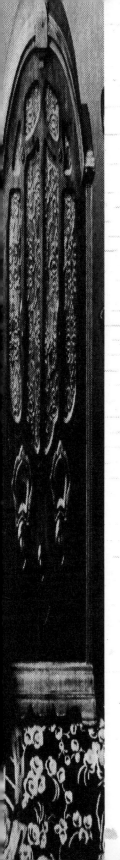

Listening to Blues

        hello

i hear the horns

        sounding up

                all 'round

blues

        blast building

                to propel me

out

        like a fly on a hook

                only to be

yanked back

        before i taste the river

                the river flowing by

bye-bye

        by to a future

                i'm not going to see

the next tune

        the same

brass, man

        whining through the sunshlne

                of another dying day,

urging me

        move away

let the rock of a train deliver me to the promise land

                the city tavern

where music is live

        and alive

                'til well after dawn

says hello

46 crowded rooms subway platforms

brushes and canvas

the heavy meditative energy of the painter's studio is
disturbed by the persistent ticking of the clock almost
imperceptibly speeding up, generating a crescendo of
rhythm threatening to shriek into a continuous thread of
nerve-twisting pulses unseparated from one another by a
silent space – a silent space where the mind can rest from
the race of competing thoughts struggling to dominate the
foremost aspects of consciousness, striving to dictate the
action beyond the tip of the brush, render the image an
expression, a taste of the essence driving the thought to
excel, surpass all thought, become something more than
chemical impulses leaping the silent spaces between
synapses . . . the mind is abandoning the steady peeling off
of layers, the quiet meditative practice, the search for a
muzzle capable of gagging thought and the clock still tick,
tick, tick, tocks.

i, the model in static repose, nod off, slide from the context
of objects into the subjective menagerie of mind in sleep.
active mind recreating images without substance – a
surrealistic narrative defying analytical deconstruction,
rational comprehension, the grasp that yearns to render it a
useful tool for sublimating emotion – mixed messages
bleeding forms together to compose a senseless reality
fantastically mimicking the scene the painter seeks to
reflect with each smooth stroke and violent jab of brushes
designed to transform the three-dimensional to two
dimensions.

the dream recurs: she is lying in the road – i am standing –
the bike is burning – a wailing like that of a shrieking child
slices the smoke; no sirens arrive.

i remember when we met and the heavy august humidity
descended to the ground, a fog thick with urban waste.
when introduced we were distracted by a pigeon with only
one eye awkwardly hopping between us on its left leg. it is
always in the dream: still hopping between her and me,
defiantly blocking my path, keeping me from saving her,
pulling her from the flames.

the dream recurs reminding me that my love is dead, that
the pigeon now coos in my helmet; that the silent spaces
are the inches of a thread persistently ticking past, wanting
to be cut.

i wonder if the painter can sense my torment, intuitively
know the realm my spirit roams, channel the energy i bring
to the studio into his soul and onto the canvas where it will
transform the study of a figure into a record revealing his
skill, my pain, the meditative energy in which we nod.

48 crowded rooms subway platforms

And

and the hacker cracks the system,
and the lawyer cracks his lobster,
and a bullet cracks a cranium,
and another pipe of crack
     cracks the addict,

and we joke about his death
     as if he is already dead,
and he laughs right along with us
     hoping the noise of his guffaws
     will hide his desperate dog
     paddle for the shore,

and there is a sign in the sky,
and a light on the ridge,
and a warning on the underside
     of each wave,

and some can see, and some are blind,
and some talk loud, and some stay mute,
and some think they care, and some know they don't,
and some will always listen to everything that is said,

and i
     i touch my last match to the wick of a candle
     so i can light cigarette after cigarette
     without having to move.

philip arima 49

Bam Bamming

wearing

        an eyeless mask

of cotton candy

           the chocolate trick

     a hazy fix,

           subtle sugars

refined, raw

           got me through childhood doors

          to adolescent scream

speed the dream

          benzedrine and

the jets thrust, thrusting

       thrusting

         a jewel filled bag

in every pocket

            black beads, christmas trees

20/20's and bright pink hearts

           bam bamming

       in the cavity

with brilliant fades

            and phasing colours

serious zones and distorting drones

         push, pushing

       pushing

         the stone virgin

dead at three

             into mindless obscurity

as the real thing

       takes command

50 crowded rooms subway platforms

describes the plan

a race through space

cadet no more

find the score

score

score

gotta call before i knock

drop a coin – dial number

repeat the ritual conversation:

hey hey how do?

good. you? fine,

real fine. coming

by? any time. after

two.

what to do   what to do   what to do   what to do

hit a bar

watch the suits

eat their lunch,

find a park

fall down crash

lose the hours

gripping cash

inside my pocket

burning like

a vic-day firecracker

dripping sweat into my eyes

at twenty-two a skeleton

praying that i'll see

at least one more

door today.

But It's Alright

with all the naivete of a saint, i easily lift open the grate. i
know better than to jump, but i do. and i go down like the
cast-out angel. i reach out, grab the icy ladder bolted to the
rock. stop – smashing my elbows and knees; biting my lip,
bruising an eye. but it's alright. 'cause it's dark and there
isn't much to see. looking up, the world seems a long, long
way away – a fuzzy circle of light. so i climb down a bit. and
i rest a bit. then i get bored and climb down some more.
and after a while of climbing and resting and climbing and
resting, i decide to jump again. and it's just the same – a
blast for the moment it lasts, but very easily forgotten. i
arrive at a ledge. stop. feel around. follow the wet wall to
where it opens on a cavity. and there i meet another. and
some others who are hanging there too. they have a fire,
some torches, shallow dry ditches in which to close their
eyes. they smell bad. and they say to me, Tell Me I Smell
Bad. so i say the same to them – become friends, speak of
things we were once going to do, and things we think we
might have done. i tell a lie. then someone else tells a
bigger lie. and someone else tells an even bigger lie. and
we all know everything is a lie. but it's alright. 'cause we're
together – living the lie. as our aimless shuffling back and
forth wears the rock floor of the cave, more join us – join us
from the shaft. some, like me, coming from above; some
from below. the ones from below look bad and don't say too
much. the ones from above get on my nerves – tell the
same lies i've already told, laugh when i cringe at the

screech of a bat dropping from the ceiling when a torch is lifted too high. but it's alright. 'cause i'm ready to leave. so i go back to the ledge. and, with all the concern of one who has undergone a frontal lobotomy, i jump. and again it's the same – not quite as thrilling, a little longer in duration, more easily forgotten. i'm hurt more when i stop. but i do it again and again and again. sometimes resting in between. until, finally, i am at the bottom – don't remember the top. and i wander around – left, then right, then left and right again. i pass shafts going down – some large, some small, all frighteningly unattractive. and sometimes i pass another, but that is rare 'cause there are very few of us down here. and we don't speak – we just skulk by one another, ready to fight if we have to, but not really wanting to bother doing much of anything. a few moments ago, i tried opening my eyes wide – wide like i think i once did when birds would fly across the sky and land on green trees, and the wind . . . the wind . . . the wind did something to me that i seem to recall felt good.

Up And Away

On the Bathurst bus,
a fragmented man
slouched across from me
(salt-marked snowmobile suit,
desperate, featherless look)
looks down the aisle
to a stranger's face
tells it:
"The spaceport
has to be
between here
and Windsor."

He looks
another place:

"Do you know where
            the spaceships land?"

No one speaks,
he looks at me.

In surplus combat gear,
black knit hat
dark glasses
hiding
eyes,

i twitch acknowledgement.

He nods
and pleads:

"I need to find a spaceship.
I need to leave,
this place is dead.
I need to leave my brain,
get away and live.

"Do you know where
                    the spaceships land?"

"I don't man,"
i say, "I don't know."

"It's here,
somewhere in Ontario. Maybe near Windsor;
far from Ottawa."

"Where do you want to go?"
i ask.

"Israel.
Up and to Israel.
Up
where it's not crowded.
Up
where there's joy in life."

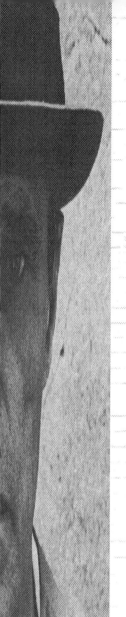

"Joy is wherever you are,"
i preach.

"Is it in Calgary?"

"If you're in Calgary."

"Is it crowded there?"

"I don't know, man.
Never been."

A woman
is staring at me,
others talk,
the bus is stuck
in traffic –
angry, honking traffic.

"How do you know
it's not crowded up there?"
i ask.

He empties his lungs,
looks down at his hands,
visibly shrinks and says:
"I don't."

There is nothing more
for us to say.
We sit alone
on the tail end
of the morning rush
bus
and i wish i had
the answer
to help this man.

"Do you know where
            the spaceships land?"

A few minutes more
and the bus pulls into the
station and people push
for the door and i stand,
take off my glasses, look over
at the still-seated man and
when our eyes connect,
i say:
            "Good luck."

            "Good luck man," he mumbles.

                        "Do you know where
                        the spaceships land?"

                        "Do you know where
                        the spaceships land?"

punk got stomped by designer boots

the inside edge lit by mirror-ball reflection
another ice-cube puddle on the floor

see me there – iron burns inside my wrists
blackening toes bound by silken threads

watch me bash my carved-up skull
against the corner farthest from the door

starve the brain, the mind will follow
hump-grinding groin and violent movement

this is not a tease or precision flirt
i'll stretch my claws and follow through

tap dance, jive, jitterbug, waltz
disco, rock, rap and break

computer components and bionic beauty
for every new bomb a luxury is built

and above the land and beneath the ocean
we eat the lies with eyes wide open

kid or tripper or voyeuristic pedestrian
last last-call is not a finish line

each revolution is part of the evolution
no single movement holds the solution

and wearing plastic shields to shut out the light
will not stop the rain leaking down my face.

58 crowded rooms subway platforms

erections, dreams and scratches

crashed,
went under deep,
fifteen hours asleep.

don't remember a single dream.

not even a vague image
or opaque emotion,
sound or scent.

down for fifteen hours sleep.

woke with scratches
on my neck
and face
chest arms legs;

all four pillows
ripped from their linen,
the fitted sheet
a tangle

and
a huge erection demanding attention.

a good fifteen hours

to forget.

philip arima 59

Typing

hitting the shift key
seems so much effort
to adhere to a system
i don't understand.
sure, the words have to scan
but the critical concern
is the ideas they signify;
bio-electric thought
to electronic thought shot
across a net, or
out a printer port.
i just want to communicate
the chaos
in the p.c. on my shoulders
without all the static
and useless software
i've collected
over years
and years
of sucking in
data.

Poems

sleep deprivation
and malnutrition
work well

relationships
or the idea of a relationship
or the thought to have an idea
of a relationship
or even a fantasy of a good one-night stand
work well

witnessing, participating in, breaking up, inciting, continuing,
losing or winning a fight
work well

a friend's failure
a rival's success
revenge, death
(provided it's not your own)
work well

funerals, parties
dancing, births
sometimes even weddings
work well

love and loving
caffeine, nicotine
caffeine – more hot black caffeine

philip arima 61

ice cream too, chocolate, strawberry
heavenly hash

running out of cigarettes
getting ill
and getting well
work well

really bad music
really good music
really loud music
really raving, raging, scintillating
late at night to all-day music
work well

terror, bliss
a first kiss
a hug
parades, zoos
walking around nude
work well

boots you can wear for three days straight
a bike with tailpipes glowing red
jacked-up trucks, supercharged cars
crowded rooms
subway stations
conversations
little children playing in the park

62 crowded rooms subway platforms

chasing dreams
a hot bath by candlelight
pillow talk
whispered words, shouted words
sentimental and angry words
words another poet writes
words that are best left unsaid
words you did not expect
each of these
when the time and timing is right
work well

quitting your job
leaving school
stopping to appreciate
breathing the air
work well

but you can never really tell, know
until you've penned the last letter
and reread the words, and
reread the words
reread the words
if
you have
actually
written
a poem.

philip arima 63

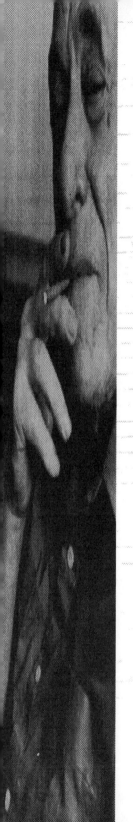

Roommates

It was February and snowing
but because it was a two-for-one sale
she bought ice cream: a brick of chocolate,
a brick of strawberry.

She brought them home and put them
in an old four-litre Good Humour container
we've had hanging around for years.

Now, i like chocolate – chocolate is one of those things
that makes me want to say: Wow.
Chocolate is what i've always eaten.

And she put the chocolate underneath the strawberry.

I had to shovel the strawberry out of the way,
dig down for the chocolate, then shovel the strawberry
back into place.

It was a lot of work for a dish of ice cream.

Anyway, there i was sitting at the kitchen table,
listening to D.O.A., reading Bukowski
and eating my chocolate ice cream
when i get a mouthful of strawberry
and discover i like strawberry too.

She must have noticed my excavation
through the strawberry to the chocolate
because ice cream is on sale again
and this time she put the strawberry
on the bottom.

philip arima 65

What Passes for Love

written by Stan Rogal
designed by Mike O'Connor

Freckles

Well, like they say: *the worst I ever had was great* and, yeah, to be honest, this time it'd been OK. It wasn't bad. It was all right. I mean, what can you expect? It's a natural progression, right? You sleep with the same person over and over and it can't always be like in the movies, all bells and fireworks. That goes without saying and you have to accept it as fact. And not only her - me too. Me too. You know, sometimes you're not quite into it, or you're tired or there's something weighing on your mind - whatever - yet somehow you want to a little bit more than you don't want to (this is you or the other person or the both of you now, you understand) or you figure it might be just what you need at the time when maybe it isn't or - who knows? And so you do. You do, and usually, for the most part, it's OK. It's nice. You do it and no one's nose is out of joint and you say goodnight in a civilized way and you roll over and go to sleep. And that's how it had begun.

We had climbed into bed and she said she'd like a little snuggle, and there had been no hint beforehand and it was the furthest thing from my mind, but I thought, sure, what the hell, why not, and I obliged, except during the whole time after she'd got me up and in, she sort of disappeared on me, you know? Like her mind was fixed on something other than the fact of me working away inside her. Which, again, was not unusual. I mean, I knew by this that she was not in the mood for an orgasm, just a snuggle, and I could enjoy myself and not have to worry about her. So I did, then rolled off and gave her a hug, a kiss; you know. It was OK, like I said. Nice. It was nothing new up until then, only this is the time she decides to tell me, while I'm lying back all comfy-cozy, relaxed and loving her, right? I mean, on the one hand, you'd think that would be the absolute worst time, but on the other, it makes a lot of sense, when you think about it. I mean, the same sort of thing happened when she banged up the car. And when she quit her job. She waited for the exact same time to tell me. And you can't blame her. I mean, there is no best time or right way. What I'm saying, I guess, is that it's something like when the cat drops a dead bird at the foot of the bed - you're sorry for the bird, but the cat's just trying to make up for something or show its affection and it's not really the cat's fault. Of course, this was something entirely different and really not in the same category at all as cars and jobs. I mean, you know what I'm talking about. This was different. This was something else and I don't have to spell it out, you understand. I mean, to tell the truth, I have a lot of trouble even thinking about it, never mind saying it. For her though, the words just spilled out. And maybe that's best too, in these situations. No fancy footwork. No beating around the bush. Just sharp and clean, like the surgeon's knife, *zip*: I've been sleeping with someone else. Just like that, she says it, and it's out in the open, hanging in the air like some kind of ... I don't know ... thing. I can't describe it. I can't begin to describe it.

You're kind of stunned at first, and then all the machinery starts in motion and it's all automatic and you've got no say in what happens after that. And this is really funny (not funny, y'know, like it wasn't funny; no one was laughing; I sure wasn't laughing; it was strange is what it was; strange-funny) because the first thing that popped into my head wasn't the first thing that I would've expected, given the circumstances. And maybe that's the way it happens all the time too, for everyone, I don't know. Maybe there's been a study, but I haven't heard of it. It's sort of embarrassing now, I guess, to say it, but the first thing that popped into my head - and remember, I had absolutely no control over this myself - the first thing was: Betty; which makes me question what the hell goes on inside a person, eh? Really. I mean, you think you've got a pretty good idea about who someone is, or a better idea about a close friend or the person you're married to, though not completely, not everything about them. So you count on a few surprises now and then, but with yourself, you figure you should know what to expect in a given situation. Right? Well, no way. I never expected this. Not in a million years. But there it was.

I started thinking about Betty and that time two years ago. I couldn't help it; I could only lay back and watch. It was her last day with the company. As the story went, she had a job lined up in Vancouver and she was hopping a plane early the next day. So the girls had prepared a little do for her in the afternoon - wine and cheese and stuff - and the guys could drop in or not. There was nothing too personal between Betty and me, we were on speaking terms and that was about it. We worked in different areas of the company, our paths crossed occasionally, we said *hello-how-are-you*; that sort of thing. Still, I stopped by and offered my best wishes. To tell the truth, I was more interested in the drinks and sandwiches. Not that there was anything wrong with Betty. She was nice enough. A bit on the quiet side; shy maybe. She wasn't my type, that's for sure. Not bad looking, but twenty pounds overweight and red hair, which never appealed to me. And *freckles*, man, did she have freckles. Her face and arms were covered with them. I don't know, I could never see myself going to bed with a woman whose breasts were freckled. Or her pussy. Don't ask why; it's just something that puts me off.

At any rate, she split early (she said she had to do a few last-minute things and finish packing) and I hung around making small talk with the rest of the girls until the wine was gone.

I was going to go home after that, but decided I wasn't in the mood. The wine had given me a bit of a buzz and I felt like continuing. Besides, the wife was out for the night taking a drawing lesson, then dinner with a friend, etcetera. Perfect. I jumped into the car and drove to a bar I knew closer to home. There were plenty of places nearby, but I like to avoid being flagged over by the cops if I can help it. Also, the job situation's tough enough as it is without being spotted by a client, or a boss or even a fellow employee. The word gets around, the story grows, and the next thing you know, you're pegged as someone with a problem. After that, it's a short walk to the unemployment line.

Anyway, I arrive at the bar and who do I see but Betty, sitting at a table in the corner, by herself and working on what turns out to be her third rum and coke. Now, I never in my wildest dreams would've expected to see her in a place like this, alone, drinking double rum and cokes, but there she was. Well, if she hadn't turned at the that moment and spotted me, I probably would've just backed out and left. I didn't want to be involved. But she did see me, so I walked over and said hello and she started crying. She had been crying but now she really broke down.

Seems she wasn't going to Vancouver after all. Her boyfriend had dumped her, she was pregnant, she had planned to go in for an abortion, except now she wasn't sure if she wanted to go through with it; like, maybe she should have the baby. You could've knocked me over. Who'd've thought it?

I tried to console her; bought her another drink, wiped her eyes, *yeah, most men are assholes* and so on and so forth, and ... to make a long story short (don't ask me how it happened, it just did) we ended up going at it in the back of her van (now that's another thing... I never much saw her as a *van* person either, but there you go) except, when it came to the crucial moment, that is, when she's made up her mind to write the boyfriend off for good and she's ready for me to slip it in, I suddenly started thinking: *What am I doing? I'm happily married. I've been married for eight years and I haven't screwed around once. Maybe toyed with the idea once or twice, that's natural, but never done it. I love my wife. I love my kids. Do I want to maybe lose it all for this? I mean, who is this woman? What is she capable of? She's in a desperate position, after all.*

So, I tuck it back in my pants. I tell her she's a bit mixed up at the moment, a bit drunk (I'm a bit drunk) and I don't want to take advantage of her and everything will work out in the end etcetera. And I zipped up and left.

I never saw her again. I don't what happened to her. She might've thrown herself in the lake for all I knew. I felt bad. I did. But what else could I do? I checked for her name in the papers for weeks. I watched for her at the bar. Nothing. No sign. So, I more or less forgot about her.

And then, the next thing, I'm lying there in bed and my wife is telling me what she told me and I'm thinking: *What a first-class jerk. Why didn't I do it when I had the chance? I could've. I should've.*

Stan Rogal 71

I was a fool not to. I mean, what a stupid, middle-class, bullshit attitude, you know? What I'm saying is, that's what I mean when I ask what goes on inside someone. I mean, what was it that made me think that way with Betty two years ago and what was it that made me think of her after my wife told me ... you know, and I was lying there? I don't know. All I know is, that's what flashed through my mind. I couldn't think of anything else, only: *You dumb bastard!*

So I got up, cleaned myself off, got dressed and walked out the door. I didn't say a word. I must've had some idea of where I was going, what I was going to do, but I'm not sure. Mostly, it was a blur. It was like I'd shifted into automatic pilot. I was totally out of touch. I certainly wasn't inside myself. No way. I was further outside myself than I think I'd ever been. It was like watching a movie of myself. One of those old home movies, all grainy and jerky.

So, what did I do? Just what you'd expect. I drove to the liquor store. Except it was closed. It had been closed for hours. I thought: *For chrissakes, what sort of anal retentive country is this that prevents someone from buying a bottle after 9 p.m.?*

Then I remembered there were a couple of bottles of red wine under the seat. I'd bought them for something. I don't know what, but sure enough, there they were! Now that's more like it, I thought. I cracked one and started guzzling. I just kept driving and drinking until the bottle was empty.

Next thing I know, I'm pulling into the parking lot of a bar - the *same* bar, mind you, which I guess is no big deal since I'd often come by since, it's just that things seemed to be adding up to something in a peculiar way. I tossed the empty into the back and tucked the full one under the front seat.

I went into the bar and ordered a scotch with a beer chaser. I knew the guy behind the bar. His name was Dave. He asked how I was doing and I told him terrific, never better. He said that's the way and gave me my drinks. I didn't want to talk. I wanted to be drunk. That's it. So drunk that I wouldn't have to face all those questions I knew were bound to arise surrounding that single statement: *I've been sleeping with someone else.* But it's like when someone you love dies. You can all of sudden consume vast quantities of alcohol to no effect. Or maybe you are affected but you don't know it. Maybe you have to rely on a second opinion to know what shape you're really in. I asked Dave.

"Do I look drunk to you?"

"Man," he said, "from where I stand, if you can ask that question you must be either very drunk or very sober."

So there you go. I finished the scotch and ordered another. I began to look around the room. There was a guy playing the piano. Not very well. A regular. I'd seen him before. There were two couples shooting pool. Another couple sat holding hands at a table. Around the bar there was an old Chinese gentleman dressed in a black suit and a white shirt. He looked like an undertaker. He was reading a racing form and sipping on a beer. Two seats away from him was a forty-fivish year old woman, skinny with too much make-up, grinning beside a young guy who was entertaining her by rolling a coin between his fingers. She'd take long drags from her cigarette, tilt her head back and blow smoke in a line toward the ceiling, where it would quietly explode.

Then I noticed, way back in a corner, in a booth, sitting alone, a red-haired woman, and I thought: no, it can't be, not after two years, not tonight. Yet, she looked familiar. I asked Dave what she was drinking and he told me double rum and cokes. He smiled. I ordered another scotch, another beer, a rum and coke and headed over.

It was Betty all right, and she recognized me. She offered me a seat, pleasant-like, as though we had just seen each other yesterday. She looked good. Thinner, I thought. We talked. Not about anything. Just talked. We ordered more drinks. I crept closer to her, or she crept closer to me. At any rate, we were soon pressed together in the booth, whispering to each other, rubbing our hands over each other's legs beneath the table. When the bar closed, Betty said she was in the mood for another drink. I told her I had a bottle of wine in my car and asked her if she still owned that van. She did. I grabbed the jug and away we went.

I thought, this time things will be different. Nothing unexpected. Last time, we were piss-eyed drunk; our clothes were half-on, half-off. I remember wanting it that way: I didn't want to see her body. I thought it might disgust me, so I'd kept my eyes closed, or else fixed on an earring or a small white area on her cheek. This time, I wanted to look. I wanted to see her pale skin swarming with reddish freckles. I undressed her slowly, undid her bra and placed my finger on a freckle that sat on her chest at the point where the breast began to swell. Then I placed my finger on another, and another. I began to count them, even though I knew it was impossible. My finger travelled slowly down and around her nipple; then to her belly, her hip, her thigh and between her legs. Her body rose toward me; she grabbed hold of me, pulled me on top and guided me inside her. I felt her freckles shift between our flesh like strange, exotic fish. At least, I imagined it was happening. It was beautiful.

When we were done, she left. There was no mention of the past, no messy questions about what we do next or where do we go from here. It had happened and it was over. I got into my car and went home. What else could I do? I pulled into the drive, parked, got out, walked up the steps, through the door, into the living room and down the hall. I pushed open the bedroom door. There was my wife, still sitting up in bed. And there, also, was me, my head tucked beneath her breasts, against her belly. We were both crying. She was rocking me in her arms, saying: *Don't cry. Don't cry.* My finger was tracing a tiny freckle on her hip. My lips were moving. I was counting.

Exhibition

Karl stepped back from the canvas and shrugged. *That's it*, he thought. *Done.* He wiped his hands with a rag, lit a cigarette, inhaled, blew a few smoke rings. He squinted at the painting, picked up a brush and made a motion or two with his wrist as if he were going to make some slight alteration. Then he changed his mind. *Fuck it*, he thought, and simply signed his name to the corner.

This was the last of twelve paintings in a series, one named for each month of the year, chronicling the change of scene outside Karl's window. It had seemed like a good idea at first. Now, he was sick of the whole thing; he'd had enough. *Just wrap the bastard, get it down to the shop and stick it with the rest.*

Tonight he was to have his first one-man exhibition in a reputable gallery with a reputable dealer. The dealer had seen samples of Karl's work hanging in a local pasta joint and gave him a call offering the show, publicity, invitations - even an opening-night celebration with wine and cheese - the whole ball of wax. Karl felt excited at the time and more than slightly flattered. It wasn't long, however, before these feelings were replaced by fear and doubt: fear that the work would be unsatisfactory or that he'd be unable to meet the deadline; doubted that his paintings would attract an audience in any case. *Who the hell would want to come out for me?* That was the question he posed to himself about ten thousand times a day. *An artist? Shit, I'm no artist. No fucking way. I never should've quit my job at the beer store. I was making a good buck. I had a fucking life. I must've been nuts.*

"Karl! Karl! Are you going to answer the door or what? Karl?" Beth charged across the room in long, determined strides. "Chrissakes, you can't even go to the can around here."

Beth was a big woman, not fat, but tall, big-boned and furnished with an abundance of good, solid flesh that she carried with comfort and grace. Her dirty blonde hair was thick and wild, managed only by Beth constantly running her hands through it. She finished zipping her fly just as she opened the door. It was Mr. Mendino, the landlord. He stood gaping in the doorway.

"Well, what the hell do you want?" Beth was about twice his size and straightened up to increase her advantage.

"Ah, Mrs. Phillips, good day." Mr. Mendino kept his eyes moving from Beth, to the floor, to the door frame, to the room of the apartment behind Beth. "Um, I wonder, is Mr. Phillips at home?" He tried to crane his neck around Beth but she leaned with him, blocking his view.

"No, Mr. Phillips isn't home. Why do you want him?"

"No, well, it's about the rent, Mrs. Phillips."

"Oh now Mr. Mendino, you know that I get paid on Fridays. That's tonight. You'll have your money tomorrow."

"I'm sorry Mrs. Phillips, but the fifteenth was yesterday. You're already a day late."

"You'll get your money tomorrow. Like I said."

"Mrs. Phillips, please ..."

"Look, will you stop calling me Mrs. Phillips. I am not Mrs. Phillips. There is no Mrs. Phillips. I am Ms. McKenzie as you goddamn well know. Just as you goddamn well know that I get paid on Fridays."

Mr. Mendino glanced down the hall. "Please, the neighbours."

"To hell with the neighbours! Maybe now they won't have to lean against the keyhole to hear me."

"Mrs. Phillips, I must warn you..."

"Warn me? Warn me about what? The cracked ceiling? The leaky taps? The broken toilet? What are you going to warn me about? The missing floor tiles you promised to replace since the day we moved in? The fucking cockroaches? Hmm? What?" Mr. Mendino's jaw tightened. "Or maybe it's not the rent you're after." Beth took a deep breath. She was braless beneath her blouse and her breasts were large and firm. She tucked the tips of her fingers between two buttons. "Maybe you don't want Mr. Phillips at all, hmm? Maybe you're wanting to work out a little trade with me. Hmm? Is that it? Is that your game?" She undid one button. Mr. Mendino backed away, almost tripping over his own feet.

"Tomorrow," he sputtered. "I expect to see the rent money tomorrow at the latest." He turned and fled down the stairs.

Beth laughed as she slammed the door. "Hypocritical little wop." She spun around and faced Karl. "Did you hear that shit? Him tryin' to threaten me? I had him peeing his pants."

Karl grabbed a sweater from the bedpost. "He's not a wop. He's Portuguese."

Beth shook her hands through her hair and approached Karl. "Same difference. They're both fucking sardine eaters." She wrapped her arms around his neck. "Anyway, what's the big deal? "

"You bullied him."

"I bullied *him*? That's a good one. What about the crap he tried to pull on me? And don't think he wouldn't love to get his greasy paws on me. Ha! He goes out of his way to give me the old hairy eyeball; you better believe he does."

"He's harmless."

"Yeah, like a rat." Beth leaned into Karl and kissed his lips. Karl was actually an inch or two taller than Beth, but because of his slim build and poor posture she appeared to be the larger of the two. "Oh, I know, honey. If I had invited him in you'd've just given him the money out of your pocket and everything would have been A-OK, right?" Karl didn't answer. "Isn't that what you'd've done? Hmm?" She kissed his cheek. "Honey?"

"No."

"No. Of course not, 'cause you don't have five hundred bucks in your pocket, right? You don't have five hundred bucks period, right? Y'see - I know that. I know that and I don't care. All I care about is you and me. Together. With a roof over our heads and food on the table and a place for you to paint. That's all that matters, isn't it honey? You and me." She slipped her tongue into Karl's mouth and directed him onto the bed. She unbuttoned her blouse. "And tomorrow Mr. Mendino will have his money and everyone will be happy again." She pulled off Karl's sweatshirt and kissed his chest. "Poor Karl. Poor, poor Karl. What would you do without me to look after you, to take care of you?" She took his hand and placed it on her breast. "Do you still love me, Karl? " She unzipped his jeans. "Do you love me?" She ran her hand beneath the elastic of his underwear. "Tell me you love me. Tell me." She kissed his neck and whispered, "Tell me."

Karl stared up at the crack in the ceiling. He knew that Beth had removed her pants; that she was naked beside him. He felt her slide down his own jeans and underwear, felt her take his erection in her hand, felt her crawl on top of him and guide it inside of her.

"I don't love you," he said. "I don't love you." He spoke into her thick hair. Beth continued to rock back and forth oblivious to the words. Karl wondered whether he'd actually spoken the words aloud or not. Perhaps he had only thought them. Perhaps he had said nothing.

"You do love me, Karl. I know you do. I know." Beth inhaled, held it, moaned, shuddered then released her breath in short, sharp gasps. She moaned again. "You do love me," her voice faded, "I know you do."

෫෪

Karl arrived at the gallery by cab and unloaded the picture.

"You did it then! Good for you! I wasn't sure you'd have it ready, but here it is." George Bernard was the dealer. "We could have gone with eleven, and would have, naturally, but it's so much better, I think, with the full complement, yes?" He hadn't uncovered the picture. "January through December, yes. An entire year; full circle, as it were. Ah, Karl, this is my assistant for the evening. You haven't met and you should, absolutely. Her name is Francine. She's from Montreal. Taking art history at the university. Plus marketing and sales, plus computers, plus who-knows-what-else."

"Nice to meet you, " Karl said.

"You too." Francine was a reasonably attractive young woman, about twenty-five, Karl guessed; slim, dark-haired, stylish - perhaps a bit too made-up for Karl's taste, but, like he always figured, *what's my opinion got to do with anything?*

"I'm enjoying your work. You have a wonderful talent for creating mood with colour. I can't wait to see the latest piece." She took the package into the back room.

"You should get to know her; her father's a great patron of the arts. Especially the paintings by *unknowns*. Filthy rich. Into pharmaceuticals, real estate and God knows. Listen, people will be arriving shortly. Pour yourself a glass of wine. Relax. Oh, by the way, is your *friend* joining you tonight?" Bernard and Beth had met only once, but it seemed to be enough for the both of them.

"No. She's ... she's working tonight."

"Ah yes. Waitress or something wasn't it?"

"She drives fork-lift in a warehouse. It's swing shift."

"Mmm. Yes. Just as well really. These things can be quite boring for the partners, what with all the attention being focused on the artist. Besides, as I recall, the two of you had differing opinions as to what a painting should be, yes?"

"Yeah, well, she kind of likes a tree to look like a tree."

"Exactly. And nothing wrong with that, God knows. Variety being the spice of life etcetera and no reason to cause problems for a relationship; no reason at all." Bernard headed for the back room. "Excuse me. A few last-minute details. Pour a drink and relax. I'll send Francine back out to you. Get to know each other."

"Thanks. I'll do that." Karl poured a glass of red wine and studied the paintings mounted on the wall. He shook his head. *Are these mine?* he thought. *They've got my name on them but I don't remember doing them. There's been some mistake. I don't belong here. Who am I trying to kid? I had a good job once. A damn good job. What was I thinking? I must've been nuts. I was nuts.*

&

As far as Karl was concerned, the opening was a farce. No one seemed interested in either him or his paintings. People came and went in rapid succession, filling up on the wine and cheese and speaking with whomever could do them the most good. Bernard performed the polite introductions, which began and ended with the quick handshake and obligatory *well done* and *good show*. But what had he expected? He didn't know. Near the end of the evening, Francine tapped him on the shoulder.

"How's it going?"

"Fine, I suppose. No one's thrown a punch."

"This is fairly typical. You get used to it."

"Mmm."

"Really, no need to worry. Everyone knows that Bernard discovers and shows only the best of the new wave. You'll be in the morning papers."

"There were reviewers here?"

"Oh yes. Some here, some not here. Doesn't matter. They'll all have to come up with beautiful words and grand theories to describe you and your work. Some of it may even be close to the truth. Take my advice: enjoy it, then forget about it."

"I see. It's business."

"Exactly. That's what they do. It's their job. Your job is to paint, and show up to perform the necessary social obligations. Anyway, there's a party up the street where I'm staying. Younger crowd. Not so formal."

"I don't know if I'm up to a party."

"Oh, you have no choice. You're the guest of honour. Besides, I'm supposed to take care of you; fill you in; introduce you. It's my job. Bernard tells me that you're practically a virgin to the art scene."

Francine was right. The new gathering was less formal and the guests were younger. In fact, the suite was choked with people leaning against walls, crashing on furniture, laid out across carpet. Everyone appeared to be smoking and the air was thick with haze. The first thing Karl did was light up, then a joint was passed his way and he took a hit. *This is better*, he thought, and started to relax. He looked around for Francine, who had gone for drinks. A woman came by holding a rolled up bill and a small mirror with half a dozen white lines running across it. Karl passed. The woman grinned, shrugged her shoulders and moved on. Another joint made the rounds. Karl took a deep drag and held it in. It was good grass and he could feel it taking effect already.

"Hear that? That's Bird. Man, he could play."

"What?" Karl turned toward the voice. It came from a slim, pale young man with watery red eyes.

"Bird, man. Charlie Parker. You never heard of Charlie Parker?" His tone was accusatory. Karl was going to say something when another voice jumped in.

"You're fulla shit, asshole. That's not Charlie Parker. That's Dexter Gordon, man. You're fulla shit."

Karl walked away, leaving the two to argue between themselves. What did it matter to him who was playing? As far as he was concerned, you either liked the song or you didn't. Parker, Gordon - what difference did it make? It was the music that counted. Like choosing between a Picasso or a Rockwell or a finger painting your eight-year-old kid did in school - you're going to hang up the one you like and that's art. Between the wine and the dope and the bullshit, Karl was feeling testy. *Yeah,* he thought, *I'm in the mood to match my ignorance against someone else's arrogance.* At that moment, Bernard rushed over with a good-looking man in tow.

"Well done, Karl. Well done. Extraordinary. It was wonderful tonight. Marvellous. Everyone was impressed. Totally, totally - impressed." Bernard burped lightly, laughed, gave the young man a squeeze around the waist and wove his way back into the crowd.

Karl noticed that the two guys arguing about the music had called in reinforcements to back their positions. *Why not just look at the name on the goddamn cover,* he thought. Then it struck him that this party was also "just business." None of these people were artists; they were the art scene. Karl looked at his hand and saw that a drink had somehow materialized. It was a large scotch, neat. He threw it back and tried to find his way to the door.

"You ready to leave?" It was Francine. "Me too. C'mon. My room is down the hall."

๛

It was all too much for Karl. He let himself be led. Francine seemed pretty high herself. She was giggling and made little sighing, snorting sounds through her nose. She dragged Karl to the bed and began to undress him.

"Is this just business too?" He had wanted to hurt someone, earlier, in the other room, but it had come out now and he was surprised and angry at himself. He was about to apologize except that Francine continued without missing a beat. Had he spoken? Had she heard? She pulled down his pants, rubbed his thighs with her hands, then gazed up at him.

"It's my business." She giggled. The snorting sounds continued. She slipped out of her clothes and the two of them jumped beneath the covers. They kissed. Karl fondled Francine's breasts and her low snorts grew louder.

"Is everything all right?" asked Karl.

"What do you mean?"

"The sounds you're making ... I don't know if you're excited or if something's, like ... wrong."

"Oh no. Everything's fine. It's when I drink, something happens to my adenoids; they swell or something and it affects my breathing. Especially during sex. But no, I'm OK."

"OK." Karl was not totally comfortable with the snorting but figured if Francine was really interested, he'd try and give her a good time. He licked her nipples and began working his tongue down her belly and between her legs. She stopped him and drew his head back up to hers.

"No. I know that you're trying to be sweet but, I just don't like it."

"No?"

"No. It ... I just ... I don't like it."

"Oh. OK."

"I should also tell you, I don't orgasm either. I mean, I do, but only when I do it myself. When I'm alone."

"Uh-huh. Listen, are you sure you want to ... you know?"

"Yes. I want to. I mean, I enjoy it and all, I just don't come. So you don't have to feel obligated to like, wait for me, or anything. Enjoy yourself whenever you're ready, you know? I'll be fine."

"Fine?"

"I mean it's all right. I enjoy a man inside me."

"You just don't come."

"No." Francine searched with her hand between Karl's legs and found him only partially erect. "It's OK. Really."

"I know, but ... " - she shoved her tongue into his mouth and pulled him on top of her. Karl stiffened and was about to enter her when she snorted.

"Your condom or mine?"

"What?"

"Did you bring a condom?"

"Well, no, I didn't. I didn't think -"

Francine rolled out from under Karl and produced a condom from the bedside table.

"This is the '90s after all. Better safe than sorry. You do wear one, don't you?" She tore open the package. Karl stared numbly. "I mean, Bernard told me that you have a partner." Francine attempted to fit the rubber but Karl's slight erection withered under her touch.

"What's the matter?"

"Nothing." Karl tugged at his short beard. "I don't know. The dope, maybe. The excitement. I don't know. I have to go."

"Maybe you just need a few minutes -"

"No. It's better if I go. Really." Karl slid out of the bed and got dressed. He crossed the room, opened the door and left without looking back.

Karl went into the bathroom, undressed, washed, then tiptoed into the bedroom. He saw Beth curled up on her side of the bed clutching a pillow, her back to him. He slipped in beside her.

"You're late."

"Mmm."

"What time is it?"

"I don't know. Aren't you already asleep? You should be asleep."

"I wanted to know how it went."

"It went OK. I'm going to wake up famous, apparently. Like in the movies."

"Yeah?"

"Yeah." He leaned toward her. "Would you like that?" He touched her cheek and felt a tear. His hand withdrew. He laid on his back and stared at the ceiling.

"What else happened? Where were you?" Her voice grew louder. It quivered. "I want to know. I ... " Her throat tightened, sealing off the words. She flipped over and placed her head on his chest. "No. I'm sorry. Don't tell me. I don't want to know. Only ... " She pushed her hair back from her eyes. They were both naked. She rubbed her breasts against his arm, reached down with her hand and got him erect. She mounted him, whispering, "Do you love me baby? Do you love me? Tell me, now. Tell me. Come on, baby." Karl remained motionless, his gaze fixed on the barely visible crack in the ceiling. He opened his mouth as if to speak, then stopped, then opened his mouth again. "Do you feel safe?" he asked.

"Safe? Is that what you asked me?"

"Yes. Do you feel safe?"

"I ... " She was nearing orgasm. "Yes. It's OK. It's my period. It's OK." She rocked gently on top of him with her head buried in his neck. "Tell me, baby. Tell me you love me," she moaned softly. Karl stared at the ceiling - at the crack. His body trembled. A few tears squeezed from the corners of his eyes. His jaw and lips moved but no words were forthcoming. The crack appeared to grow bigger. *Do you feel safe?* he thought. *Do you feel safe?* Beth trembled; she breathed deeply. "Tell me baby. Tell me. Tell me. For God's sake ..."

A Taste for Apricots

There is a knock at the door. Perhaps a knock. Then again, it might merely be a trick of the weather. It often happens. The wind teasing the brass ram's head, the cold dragging a shudder from the bones of an ancient oak beam. Perhaps an object's dull response to some physical law - *gravity*, we call it, knowing full well that it doesn't exist. The simple attraction of a lesser body to a greater body. Perhaps a memory spun from the juke-boxed mind by a quarter so long rubbed between the fingers that both faces are blank. Perhaps a wished-for knock that repeats at precisely the same time night after night until one is drowned senseless to any real knock and whoever stands outside finally grows weary and moves on. Meanwhile, one sits alone and wonders: do they really exist, all those unknocked knocks? Or is it only at the point of contact, knuckle on wood?

He remains frozen in mid-action, like a photograph of himself, waiting for - either the telling silence or the repeated tattoo - waiting for the cue which will reanimate him, cause him to follow through with the interrupted movement (though, with a difference), or substitute a new action altogether. Years pass in this brief instant as an infinite number of stories shuffle and re-shuffle. This is not a projection. The lines in his face indicate the process clearly, even as the steam issuing from the pot on the burner acts to destroy the illusion of timelessness. Then it occurs, as surely as if it were planned - the knock. He drops the lid onto the pot and hurries to the door, his hand hesitating a moment, his body drawing a deep breath, swallowing, before turning the handle.

"Hello." A woman stands on the porch. She isn't easy to describe but she is there nonetheless. She has no traits of extreme beauty or ugliness; no limpid-pool eyes or shock of golden tresses, no distinguishing marks or scars. If she was never the school beauty queen, she was never the school hag either. Average, perhaps *too* average and it may be specifically this that makes her appear interesting: her flagrant averageness. In the background, a fence, a road, a few trees, a field of corn, a low-rising hill, all turn violet in the afterglow of the setting sun. She, on the other hand, brightens in the warm electric glow of the porch light, separates herself from her

Stan Rogal 85

surroundings and becomes more real. She is slightly underdressed for September, he thinks.

"I've been walking for miles. I must've taken the wrong turn somewhere. Would you be able to put me up for the night?" He doesn't answer.

"A piece of floor is fine. I'm comfortable anywhere." He stares vacantly at her.

"I'm afraid I don't have any money." The two face each other and, as no other words are forthcoming, he steps aside. She enters, removes her pack and coat, places them on the couch and sits. He follows her every move, never taking his gaze away. He circles her as she gathers in the surroundings. Neither speaks. The room is silent except for his carpeted steps and the creak of an odd floorboard. He stops over one loose board, looks down at his feet and shifts his weight up and down, playing the board like a musical instrument. He looks across at the woman, smiles, shrugs his shoulders. They both laugh.

Steam explodes from the pot, rattling the lid and hissing through the ribs of the burning element. No one makes a move. The woman turns her head toward the pot, watches the water boil over. The man pulls his lower lip with his fingers then motions halfheartedly with his head, stuck somewhere between the woman and the pot. He clears his throat and mumbles.

"That's the vegetables." She nods and he walks to the stove, one eye still on her. "I was just about to eat. Are you hungry? Would you like to join me?" He doesn't wait for an answer. Even as he speaks he sets another place at the table. "There's plenty. I've roasted a chicken. There's potatoes and carrots. I always make enough for two, that is, for leftovers. Makes things easier, you know? There's even some wine. Apricot. Homemade." He fills two glasses. "Yes? Good! Umm, why don't you come and sit here." He pulls a chair slightly away from the table. "You must be tired if you've been walking for some time, I mean you must be tired." She sits in the chair and sips her wine.

"I'll serve." Provided with a practical task, his voice and manner liven, though with an urgency that seems out of proportion to the situation. He speaks as one who is afraid not to speak, as if only the presence of words is strong enough to hold the world together.

"White meat, I bet? Yes? I knew it. Or at least, I thought so. I had a feeling. You understand. Besides, it works out perfectly that way. I prefer dark, myself. I eat the white, of course, usually in a sandwich or something. With lots of mayonnaise. But I prefer dark. The potatoes are roasted as well... like the chicken. They're my favourite. Roast potatoes. And there's gravy. Not out of a can. Real gravy. You like it on the meat as well, right?" He pauses, speaks lower, slower. "That is right, isn't it? You do like gravy on the meat?"

"Yes."

"Yes? Good. Gravy on the potatoes and the meat." He grins. "But *not* on the vegetables. Right?"

"That's right."

"Good! You do like carrots, don't you?"

"Carrots?"

"I could cook up a second vegetable. There's some cauliflower in the fridge."

"Carrots are fine."

"I didn't cook the cauliflower because it's white and there's so much white on the plate already."

"Carrots are splendid."

"You're sure? I have canned peas or corn. Wouldn't take a minute to heat up." He heads for the cupboard. "I realize they're not as tasty or nutritious as when they're fresh but..."

"No, please!"

He stops. "...they're the right colour."

"Don't go to any extra trouble. Carrots are perfect."

"It's no trouble. Are you positive? I wish I had some asparagus but I'm afraid I finished it off last night." His voice stumbles, choked with the threat of tears. "I'm, I'm sorry. I wanted this dinner to be special. I'm sorry."

"There's no need. You couldn't have known. Anyway, I prefer carrots. Honestly."

"Over asparagus?"

"Absolutely. You couldn't have chosen a more appropriate vegetable. For the colour. Orange is such an indulgent colour."

"Yes?"

Stan Rogal 87

"Of course. Orange complements everything while requiring no complement itself. It is self-sufficient and complete, so able to give unselfishly and without end."

"Does that make it indulgent?"

"Orange indulges its own orangeness."

"A very lonely sounding colour: orange."

"Perhaps." They both laugh. She fills their glasses; he serves food and they eat. There is no conversation. He eats slowly, his attention focused more on her and her movements than on his food. Her eating is steady and involved, with only the occasional glance in his direction. As she eats, her food divides into separate piles of chicken, potatoes and carrots which she tends to work down evenly until she reaches a last forkful of potato. She wipes up the remaining gravy on her plate with the potato and slips it into her mouth. Before she has a chance to chew it, he calls:

"Wait!" She freezes, her eyes fixed squarely on him. "There's something there," pointing at her lips. "A hair, or something." She slides her tongue out and as she does so he snatches the potato from her mouth and eats it. His eyes lower to his own plate, which is still half-full, then across to hers. She dabs her lips with her napkin. He rises slowly, takes her plate to the stove and makes up a second smaller helping. He returns to the table smiling.

"You've got a big appetite. That's rare in a woman these days. Most women I know pick at their food. Even the ones who don't diet. It seems more out of a politeness, really. A sense of politeness. As if it's rude to eat, to show hunger. I like a woman with a healthy appetite, who isn't afraid to eat; enjoys her food. Of course, you said that you had walked a lot today, isn't that right? And you got yourself lost and that's how you ended up here, on my doorstep. By accident. Walking." He pauses. "I mean, that would certainly explain your hunger. All that walking. All that exercise. Just the thing for building an appetite; sharpening the taste buds. People should actually walk more. It would do a world of good. Of course, it's difficult for some. More difficult for others. In fact, it's not a simple thing at all, for most folks. It's just too, too, I don't know - impossible? What I mean is, it just starts out sounding like such a simple thing, when, in reality, it isn't so simple at all, is it? It's difficult. There are so many things, really, that are against it, that stand opposed to it that one well, what I guess I'm saying is, you can plan it for years and years, right down to the last detail, and never step foot outside your door. Which isn't to say that isn't the best thing in the end, after all. Considering the objections and such. The difficulties. The risk involved. It probably is the best thing for all concerned. In the long run." She cleans up her plate, takes a deep breath, lays down her napkin and sighs. She smiles. "It's only my opinion, naturally. I don't claim to be an expert." She pushes away her plate and clears a piece of food inside her cheek with a crooked finger. "You were starving. When did you eat last?"

"This morning, I suppose."

"You suppose? You don't remember?" She leans back in her chair and surveys the room.

"You have a lovely place. Do you live here alone?"

"Yes. What about you? Where are you from?"

"But you were married at one time."

"Yes. Years ago. Where were you going when you landed here?"

"What happened to her?"

"Left me for someone else. A travelling salesman. Like in the jokes. Are you on holiday?"

"That's too bad. Children?"

"Dead. There were two of them, a boy and a girl. They drowned in a boating accident. Though at the time there was some talk of foul play. Suspicion fell on their mother, my wife. She wasn't well at the time. There were some problems." He laughs a small laugh. "Stupid, right? To believe that a mother could drown her own children?"

"I remember seeing a child once - a boy or a girl, it doesn't matter - wearing a t-shirt that read: If you love something set it free. If it comes back, it is yours to keep. If it doesn't come back, hunt it down and kill it."

"What is that supposed to mean?"

She hesitates. "Nothing. It's just something I saw."

"Who are you?"

Her voice and manner brighten. "Dinner was delicious. Did your mother teach you how to cook?"

"Necessity taught me. Why won't you answer any of my

questions?"

"What?"

"You expect me to tell you everything about myself and refuse to tell me anything about you. Why?"

"It's unimportant."

"To who?"

"To me. Unimportant and uninteresting. It bores me to talk about myself."

"I see. Well, will you tell me your name at least, so I know what to call you?"

"Miriam."

"Miriam? Are you sure?"

She regards him squarely. "What an odd question."

"I mean are you sure that your name is Miriam and not Judith or Kathleen?"

"Whatever. If Miriam doesn't suit you, pick another. Am I sure? What is there to be sure of? Especially with something so common as a name."

"Don't be angry."

"I'm not."

"No. You're not. I can see that. You never get angry. And if I asked you to leave now, you would, wouldn't you? Without a fuss? Without question?"

"Yes."

"And if I asked you to stay, to spend the night here with me, in my bed, to make love with me, you'd also agree?"

"Yes."

"Why?"

"Because you want me to."

"That's all?"

"Isn't that enough?"

"Is it true - you remember nothing?" She takes her wine and sips it. He speaks quietly, as if to himself, yet audible enough for her to hear. "Not the smallest sign of recollection. Not caring, not even curious. It seems impossible. Who are you? What are you? A ghost? A witch? Some crazy escaped from the funny farm?"

"Shall I leave?"

"No. No, I want you to stay. This time - you do understand - this time, I want you to stay." She remains attentive, seemingly unmoved. "Do you have any idea what I'm talking about?" No reply. "Do you recognize me? Do you remember ever being here before?" Her tongue and lips make slight smacking sounds as she drinks. "You don't even try. You don't even make an effort. Doesn't it matter to you what happened three years ago or fourteen months ago? Doesn't it bother you that you can't remember when you last ate; where you were?"

"No. What matters is that I'm here now; that I'm full now."

"And tomorrow?"

"Tomorrow is a long way off. Whatever is going to happen will happen."

"And what has happened?"

"What has happened is past. Nothing to be done for it."

"No looking forward and no looking back and a bed for the night." His tone is harsh, though cautious.

"It suits me."

"It should frighten you. How do you know you won't be beaten or killed? Won't be raped some night or catch some sort of disease?"

"I don't. How do you know?" He sags into his chair. His mouth hangs open, moving, attempting to form words without the benefit of sound. He wipes his face with his hand and pulls at his jaw, massaging the faulty mechanism, coaxing the breath from his locked chest. Words tremble from his lips.

"Three years ago you showed up in pretty much the same way as you did this time; wearing a packsack, your hair wind blown, tired, hungry, a bit dirty. You called yourself Kathleen. Told me your car had broken down somewhere on the road; that you'd lost your way searching for a short cut. We didn't talk much. It didn't seem necessary. I fed you dinner. We drank apricot wine, put on a fire. We slept together. It seemed right, natural. The next morning we had planned to drive into town, to a gas station, then find your car. I wasn't convinced of the broken-down car story in the first place, but it was a plan of action, a way to be with you. When I woke up, you were already gone. I went into town anyway, made a few inquiries. No one could help. You had vanished. I let it drop. At least, I thought

I let it drop. But I couldn't. I couldn't forget you. I started imagining the sound of your knock at the door. As though your knock was recognizable from the rest." He chuckles. "The number of bruises I've received running to answer your knock... anyway, some nights more than others I'd feel that you would return, and so I'd turn on the porch light. There'd be signs, you know: the sound of a bird, the discovery of a lost object, the arrangement of the sheets on the bed, the smell of apricots. Or maybe nothing so tangible. A memory that drops so quickly through the mind that it's just the memory of a memory: unrecognizable, yet enough to cause a quiver up the back, in the stomach. At some point I gave up on premonitions and left the light on every night, hoping, I suppose, that I could draw you to me, like a moth. Fourteen months ago, you were back." Without room for a break, she picks up the thread of the story and continues.

"It was July. The evening simmered with a dryness you could taste, brittle and tawny as straw. I walked to your door, it was still so bright it was impossible to tell if the light was on. I knocked. When you answered, I asked for a glass of water. You seemed surprised. I wondered if I was interrupting something or if my appearance was somehow displeasing. I pushed my hair back with my hand and shook my head. Dust filled the air, I couldn't breathe, I faltered. Whether from dust or fatigue or both, I was off-balance. You took my arm and led me inside. I drank some water, slowly. The slowest glass of water I had ever drunk. You invited me to stay for dinner. We drank apricot wine cold from the fridge. The heat was stifling, still, I asked you to put on the fireplace, and you set a few sticks burning. I suggested we remove our clothes and wash each other with damp towels, watching the flames glow orange across our wet bodies. We spent the night on the floor, drinking wine, making love and washing each other with soft, coloured towels and buckets of fresh, cool water." She takes a long draft of her wine, finishing the glass. He pours more from the bottle. "Is that the way it went?"

"Something like that. At any rate, the next morning, once again you were gone." She dampens the rim of her glass with her finger and causes it to sing.

"I was hoping it would be different this time. That you had come to stay."

"Stay? You mean forever?" She silences the glass, removing her finger and licking the tip. "That's impossible."

"Why? Are you afraid that after three days you'll turn into a pumpkin or something, like in the fairy tales?"

"Is that so unbelievable?"

"Can I ask you a question?"

"Isn't that what you've been doing?"

"You think I ask too many questions?"

"I think you expect too many answers."

"Look at me."

"I am."

"I mean, look at me closely, deeply. Look at me and tell me: who am I?"

"You mean you don't know?"

"I thought I did. But that was year ago, hundreds, thousands of years ago. Now, I'm not sure." He sighs and rubs his eyes with his palms. "When I was younger, in high school, you know, sixteen or seventeen, my friends - the guys - would play a sort of game. It was a sexual game, of course, and there was a point system involved that depended on how far you got with a girl. I can't remember all the details but it was very elaborate: say, a point for holding hands, two for a kiss, three for necking, four for rubbing her breast - and it had to be real rubbing, not a kind of accidental brush - five gets the bra off, six or eight diddles her ... you get the idea - right up to ten where you actually ... " He makes quote signs in the air with his fingers, " ... fucked her. It was all based on the honour system," he laughs. "A rather strange use of the word, considering the circumstances, I suppose. Nevertheless, we'd get together after anyone had had a date or an encounter and hear the story and figure out the points. But there were also ways to lose points. This, of course, kept the game competitive, which was a problem for me. I liked being with the guys, being part of the group and listening to the stories, but I found it difficult to participate in the game. Except, to be a part of the gang meant having to be part of the game. You see, points were taken off if you went so many days without making an attempt to score." He gulps down his wine and pours more.

"I mean, not all of the guys were what you'd call movers, but I was the only one who lost so many points that I was forever in the negatives. I was starting to get a reputation that maybe I was queer or something." He chews the corner of his fingernail, concentrating his eyes on his knuckles.

"Anyway, there was this one girl - I mean, if you were in need of a few easy points by the end of the week - there was this one girl who'd go all the way after a few shots of lemon gin. She knew the game. It didn't matter to her. Who knows, maybe the girls played the same game. Or their own variation. It doesn't matter. The guys were egging me on; joking. They threatened to kick me out of the group. Called me a fag, a homo. You know how cruel kids can be. So I asked her out, bought a bottle of gin from the local bootlegger, borrowed the old man's car and took her to some secluded back road. I didn't want to be surprised by the arrival of my pals checking up on me. We parked and started drinking right out of the bottle. We didn't talk. I stared at her rather stupidly. I wanted to get it over with and I didn't even know how to start. So I just stared at her. She wasn't pretty, kind of gawky and angular, all edges, but she wasn't ugly either. Everyone called her 'carrot top' or 'freckles'. Even the girls." He pauses, shakes his head as if to clear it.

"Anyhow, we drank some more gin, until we both had a nice glow on and things felt kind of dreamy. Then she lifted her ass off the seat and hiked up her skirt. She wasn't wearing underwear and I figured this is it, she'll just say: 'OK, big boy (or some other cliche), stick it in, get your rocks off, score your points and take me home.' Simple." He grabs the wine glass in both hands and brings it to his nose. He sniffs the bouquet. His eyes take in the woman.

"Except it wasn't like that. She grinned and pointed between her legs saying: 'If you want this, you'll have to do something for me first.' " He places the glass to his lips and drinks. "She wanted to make love. I mean, really make love. She guided me through and it was beautiful, not like the stories I'd heard at all; gentle, caring. And frightening. When it was over, I didn't know what to do or what to say. I wondered whether she had been like this with all the other guys or only with me, but I was afraid to ask. Meanwhile, she got dressed as though nothing had happened. She picked up the condom I had brought for the occasion off the floor and tucked it - still in its plastic wrapper - in my shirt pocket. Suddenly, I hated her. I hated her, because, while it was over for her, for me it had just begun. I wanted to lash out at her; hit her, smash her face in, call her names: slut, pig, whore. To free myself, you understand? To escape. Instead, I did nothing. I kept it inside. All the way back to her place we never spoke. I raced off, finished the gin and tried to throw up on the side of the road. I couldn't. I couldn't even get sick." There is a long silence in which the two do not move; their eyes meet. "How do you manage it?"

"What?"

"Living."

"I just... live."

"No secret, no magic formula?"

"I forget myself. I feel I am what happens in the room I'm in - not something else."

"Hmm. Sounds simple enough. But then, the impossible always does."

She gets up out of her chair and walks behind him. "What colour is the wall in front of you?"

"White."

She covers his eyes with her hands. "What colour now?"

"Still white?"

"Wrong. It's cream. Describe what's on the wall. "

"It's bare?"

"Wrong. There's a picture. A seascape. Now do you see it?"

"Yes?"

"There's a boat. What colour is it?"

"Brown?"

"Wrong. It's green. How many fishermen in the boat?"

"Two?"

"Wrong. Three. What are their names?"

"This is ridiculous. How can I know the names of three people in a picture? In a picture that doesn't even exist?"

"A minute ago you agreed it did exist."

"What if I did? Anyway, it doesn't matter which three names I give you, you'll only tell me I'm wrong, right?"

"Poor boy. You turn every statement into a question. Names are

Stan Rogal 95

less important than your ability to convince." He tears her hands from his face and spins around in his chair, holding her tight, his head pressed against the side of her hip.

"Now you describe for me the wall behind you."

"There is no wall. There is a field of marigolds that stretches to the horizon. An ocean of dazzling orange that robs the sun and coats the sky in a pane of blue ice. The only clouds crawl ponderous as dinosaurs within that frozen cube, their eyes clenched against the frost. Meanwhile, beneath their feet, a million miles away, the field undulates, weighed down by its own hot breath like some sleepy dragon. Bees make their floating buzz from flower to flower, as does the occasional hummingbird. Between the steaming land and the crystal sky a breeze perfumes the scene and the odour is not of one thing or another. It is less a sensation of smell than one of touch. One feels it - thick and humid - a pungency that clings to the skin and crawls in through the pores. The internal organs melt, the bones melt, the flesh melts, the skin burns to fine golden ash that scatters and loses itself among the marigold petals." He has released her hands and is sobbing, his tears flowing freely, staining her jeans. She cups his head, stroking his hair. He wraps his arms around her legs, buries his face in her belly, gently kisses the soft "V" formed above her legs: the pubic area, hip bones and navel; his hands caressing her thighs, massaging her buttocks, the small of her back; allowing himself to be raised, by the slight pressure of her fingers, out of his chair, kissing in turn her breasts, neck, cheeks, ears, eyes, nose and finally, her mouth.

She wakes to the sound of a nail being pounded into the outside of the window frame. She gets out of bed and goes to the door. She tries the handle, it turns, but the door is bolted shut. She lingers a moment, fingers the lock, leans her face against the wood, then returns to bed. She sits, regards her naked body, runs a hand along her amber skin, holds an arm up to the light and squints. She collapses back onto the pillow and covers herself with the sheet.

When the door bolt slides open, she doesn't budge. He enters with a tray, closes the door, and secures the bolt.

"Good morning. I've brought you breakfast. I understand your not wanting to talk to me; to look at me. I do. But you have to understand as well, from my point of view, it can't continue like this, with you coming and going. I can't bear it... a few hours of happiness compared with months and years of sadness. I want you here with me; always. You'll see, everything will turn out for the best. I have to have you. You have to stay. It isn't right, you see, what you're doing. It's no life."

He sets the tray down beside her on the end of the table and sits on the bed. He strokes her forehead. She doesn't respond.

"I'm right about this. You have to believe me. You have to understand. I'm going crazy. I can't live without you. Since you left I've dreamed the same dream night after night. Shall I tell you?" She closes her eyes; a small tear presses from beneath the lids.

"I'm searching for you. Looking everywhere, asking everyone I meet. No one knows anything about you. No one's seen you. Scenes race by like a movie going in fast-forward. I only catch glimpses. Places I've never been to, faces I've never seen. At least, nothing I can remember. Suddenly, I'm being led down a hallway. I can only see the back of the person leading me - a woman in some type of nurse's uniform. Her hand waves me past numerous heavy, locked doors. Finally, we stop and enter one of the cells. In the corner is a woman all bunched up in a grey gown, her face against the wall, covered by her arms - her bare arms pale, except for a pattern of garish specks." He wipes a tear from his cheek. "That's all I can make out: her arms and, of course, her hair." He wraps a lock of her hair around a finger. "Hair much like yours, tangled and rusty, like a mass of copper wire left too long in the elements. The nurse taps the woman's shoulder to get her attention and as she turns toward me ..." he bites his lip, "As she turns to face me, I cover my eyes. I can't tear my hands away. I can't force myself to look at her. I'm too afraid ... too afraid. Then the dream is over. I wake up."

"Are you afraid that the face you will see will be mine?"

"No. I'm afraid it will be my own."

"I also have a dream. I dream that I am a shoe surrounded by a world of feet. The feet want to wear me, naturally. They try to slip into me, but none fit. I'm either too big or too small. Still, they keep at me, not knowing what else to do."

"Is that really your dream?"

"No. I made it up. I never dream."

"Your breakfast is getting cold. I'll leave you now." He walks to the door and unlocks the bolt. The door opens, behind him is a crash of glass and cutlery on the floor. She remains lying on the bed, her head rolled on the pillow, facing him as he slowly turns.

"Why do you hate me so?" Her voice is low, but clear. He steps out of the room and closes the door. The bolt slides shut.

"I've brought you a bowl of apricots." He sets the bowl on the end table and cleans up the previous day's breakfast off the floor as he speaks. "I know how you love apricots. I remember the one time when there were fresh apricots on the table and you picked out one to eat - picked out, mind you, as though it was the best of the bunch. Almost as if, rather than you choosing it, it had chosen you. You didn't eat it right away. Instead, you held it in your palm, stroked its fur with your fingers as though it were a tiny animal. You raised it to the light, studying every smooth line, seemingly fascinated by its shape, entranced by its colour. Then you transported it to your mouth as a kind of offering. You closed your eyes, your lips parted - I could tell you were tasting it even before your teeth had penetrated the flesh, before your tongue had tasted the juice. And it wasn't just a pleasure of the mind, you were able to enjoy it with your entire body. It was hypnotic. Watching you, I couldn't help but think that the flavour of the actual apricot would be a disappointment. I was wrong. You bit into the fruit and it was like ... like ... I don't know. I can't describe it. I don't have the words. There are none. I wanted to cry. I guess that's what it was like." He takes an apricot from the bowl.

"I love the way you handle an object. The way you examine it. You have the marvellous ability to make the simplest things precious.

I love watching you eat." He holds the apricot beneath her nose. She doesn't move. She refuses to even sniff at it.

"Please. You must eat something." He rubs her lips lightly with the fruit. "Please." He lays it on her pillow. A hand emerges from the sheet. She takes the apricot and slowly lifts it up to the light. He stands back to watch. She poses like this for a moment, then releases her grip. The apricot drops to the floor.

"Yesterday my skin was tanned. The light barely penetrated. Today it's like rice paper. I can see every vein. By tomorrow morning I'll be a puff of smoke and by evening a ghost smothered among the white sheets." Her arm snakes back beneath the covers. He drags himself out the door.

He stands trembling in the doorway, eyeing her form, motionless except for a faint shiver of breath. A column of light breaks across her body, blurring the sharp edges of her skin and stoking her wild hair to flames. He pushes the door, the handle bangs against the wall. He turns, walks to the living room and sits in a chair facing away from the front door. He picks up a cloth and a rifle and polishes the barrel. Sounds filter from the bedroom: the creak of bed springs, the shuffle of feet, the slap and zip of clothing being put on, the march of boots moving without hesitation out of the bedroom, through the living room, down the hallway, the opening of the door and the final click. He carries the rifle into the bedroom and crosses to the bed. He sits on the edge, the butt of the rifle set between his legs. On the pillow lie three apricots, split in half, their stones removed. He reaches out a hand and traces a finger around the moist edge of each apricot section. He licks the tip of his finger. The rifle slips from his grip and falls to the floor. He crawls into bed, rests his head on the pillow, closes his eyes, and slowly, indulgently, devours each apricot, one by one.

Stan Rogal 99

Between the Ocean
and the Moon

by Tatiana Freire-Lizama

designed by Cara Scime

Waiting through night for the long, long day

IN THE TIME of the long day it began like this:
without a start or middle, there was no end.
The sun a fixed stare, eye of the blue canopy.
The galaxy settled and stayed, face
to the light, still as sleeping infants.
That was all.

Then we made the first mistake: you
aimed a branch and your lover's head
gave gently at its seams, or, who knows
maybe I gave birth to a child without hands
and suffocated him gently under
a pile of autumn leaves. Or he lived
and invented the word, "power".

And clearly, something would change.
We sniffed, noses to the earth.
We watched the sky, waiting for something to fall.
And something did fall; the sun.
The bodies of heaven jarred to a start,
lurched once like a colt's first run, and spun.
There could be no more stillness.

The first night we spent in blindness and terror of cold.
We gave day a name and prayed to it.

Light's return was round with promise, but the second night
stunned our celebrations. It was several months
before we believed the routine.
Meanwhile, the intensity of dark
drove some to hallucinations
and those were the first of us to dream.

The long day has not returned. Each night
our realities are murdered and must rise again,
each break of morning, a second chance
granted endlessly. Night hinges still
on the afflicted day.

We face choices: dissolve our hate
to stave off night. Nurture it, and bring on
the longest of long nights (we will descend
and dream always). Or, continue this slow
ebb and tide in fine increments: one night
our minds will be wiped clean in sleep,
we will spend our lives learning to speak
a language born with us daily.

Bad Words

Hay palabras que, sofocadas, hablan más – Gabriela Mistral

Some words
speak louder if you muffle them.
They are not forceful words
of themselves; they have no
eagle talons to rip and tear or
beaks sharp as the condor's to break
marrow from bone. They do not charge
as bears do, they lack
the idiot hunger.

They are fleeting, these words, thin
as mist, scattered like daylight
in woodlands. Shout them against wind, whisper them
to the ebbing tide, and they return as echoes
that echo themselves endlessly.
In constant flight, they gain shape on the wing,
become hardened and corporeal.
Everyone who makes their contact
bears their mark.

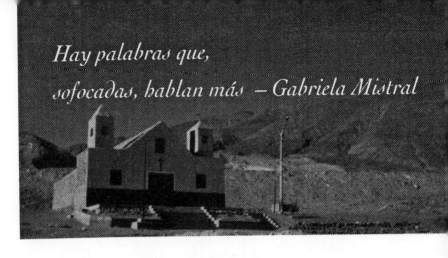

Hay palabras que,
sofocadas, hablan más — Gabriela Mistral

For some, they are an embarrassment,
words in outrageous clothing that wink
suggestively at men on the street, won't
leave their shoes at the door, refuse
to wear deodorant. Words like these
are apt to make phone calls to wives
in the middle of the night, turn up
drunk at funerals and vomit at your feet.

For others, these words when written
will burn through paper. These words
are combatants in war and
will drag you in among their enemies.
They are words that must be saved
for after curfew, and even then spoken carefully
as though with a mouthful of razor blades.
(Words like equality or peace.
Simple words we know mostly
by their absence.)

There are some words that can't be muffled,
words that we can beat and beat
and they will never do anything
but tell us their own names each time more clearly.

A Mestiza Talks About Settling America

Half of me came over the ocean
willing to die of scurvy and hunger for
God or Queen or a handful of peppercorns.
Half left warm women or
cold jail cells.
Some planned
to turn their skin to silk and return covered in saffron,
while others wanted only
to lose themselves in opiate sleep or dreams of water.

While we waited and died,
raped each other on those all-male boats,
the other half of me
went on: made love,
fought, fed children
corn ground between round stones
and offered trinkets to the rain god.
Often the trinkets were not my best
and there was not enough rain.
At night, sometimes, it grew quite cold.

Our scouts saw your sails like
giant birds, reported it as a sign
of hope. We thought it must be Quetzalcoatl,
the pale god returned from the east
but some of the advisers said
if he comes with an army, we fight him,
god or no.

It is difficult sometimes, this split
life. The tenuous ceasefire I hold
between conqueror and conquered
between victimizer and survivor or
dinner guest and the skeletal remains of a child.

And there were my two halves again,
initiating battle, balancing the sides.
There was Aguilar, abandoned
by an earlier ship or flight of swallows, maybe,
who learned our languages. And Malinche of changing colours,
said to be in love with the Conqueror but likely
just a woman who foresaw how things would be.

If you care to look, I've been in this all the way through.
I fought Aztecs, Incas, Araucanos.
And I turned on Spaniards
with hatred fed by the need
to survive.
I carried bunches of bananas
like bound-up bundles of stacked green hands
for the United Fruit Company and
plotted at night how best to break the union.
Now you'll find me as you dig
for the skeletons of children
in the mountains of El Salvador.
You can also pour me wine
dressed for dinner at the general's mansion.

It is difficult sometimes, this split
life. The tenuous ceasefire I hold
between conqueror and conquered
between victimizer and survivor or
dinner guest and the skeletal remains of a child.
Sometimes I talk to myself, get haughty, say
I discovered you. Then quickly reply,

I already knew I was here.

Great-Grandmother Lived Well

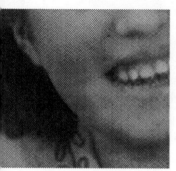

Great-grandmother lived well, she
held the world between gold-capped teeth.

He – well he was a gambler and hard
drinker, swept her off her unshod feet in a
frenzy of hope, short-lived as
dust devils on the desert roads.
By her 100th birthday the bride
could tell with equal candour the nights of love
and ones that ended in fractured bones and
small cuts to be hid from neighbours.

Great-grandmother says god took her side.
Her husband was offered her, an old man undone
by disease that shook his thick fingered hands
far worse than fear ever shook hers.
If she recalled her splintered jaw, he was not fed. Or if it was
his force on drunken nights, how she hid her face to pass
his endless line of women on the street, she let him
sit and stew in his own muck sometimes for hours.

Great-grandmother held the world
between her teeth.
When she laughed, it rolled in her mouth
like Great-grandmother took all the world had, and gave it back.
She had the world tied up
like a lamb with its feet to a post, in knots,
swinging to the feast.
She had it staring quietly at the cosmos with
its round, unblinking eye.

Great-grandmother buried two children in her teens
and felt the loss as keenly
when her others went
at 60, at 85. She said she'd had
not enough time to mourn a child
who lived for a few hours
a century before.

But great-grandmother lived well, she saw
all the gradations of light at dusk, she picked up
love with all the spills of toddlers, she knew
all the same things that oceans do, having
turned and rolled as far and as persistently.

Great-grandmother held the world between her teeth.
When she laughed, it rolled in her mouth like an errant marble.
She died from too much laughter, a shiny tumour small
and round, that lodged like a memory inside her head.

Aspects of Loss

Because the abortion was only
half successful, because it only made roomier
the space of warmth and shadow
once shared with her twin,
my mother was born to loneliness that couldn't be assuaged
and a double allocation of possibilities for pain.

She deferred in all things to her potential sister.
Took the smaller portions of dessert, wore
the shoes with the worn soles
and after a last, long look
left the tangled passions of literature,
closed herself tight and clinical, surrendered candles
for brash white lights and studied medicine.
Even my father was the second of two brothers.

She is shadowed everywhere
by a parallel reality, its entrance
eased shut like an eyelid or a
grimly smiling mouth.

I was scraped, not from her body,
but from the deep, protective flesh
of a continent. Unsuspecting and
without defence, for years I clung
to the opaque blue cord of return.

I am also trailed by the tight-lipped line of
a world of spectres, rites of passage that took
an unexpected turn. At any time,
I can step gingerly between this life and
a universe of loss, leave behind
not even the echo of recent laughter, just
a doorway closing like a neatly healing wound.
The other side is full of faces possible
only in futures and dreams brought on by fever.
Curled reading in shadows,
a woman who looks like my mother.
Behind her, one who could be me.

**Loss cannot be seen all at once; it cuts
with many faces, like a gemstone.
It begs for answers:
Once the wing is broken,
where does the condor's flight go?
Or the distance we planned to Iquique
when sleep overtakes us in Valparaíso?**

The Mountains Back Home

What's left to say about mountains?
You know how they feel
misty cool and bluish in a morning
despite the sun flashing off snow caps
that never cease to startle.
There they are. You know the ones I mean.

Maybe I'll tell you instead about the glory
of clotheslines intersecting them everywhere from this angle:
workshirts, old housedresses, grey t-shirts
wrinkled from wringing and flapping somewhat
desperately against their pins.

Or about square patchwork
hovels, corners sinking into mud
and women who trudge the paths between,
cracked hands kneading the smalls
of their thick-set backs in anticipation
of still more time at the laundry tub,
or perhaps waving impatient from his ragball gang,
a skinny kid whose ready smile
converges in overlapping front teeth.

You may never have heard
remarked against a backdrop of mountains,
Was a good dog, that one, but got rabies so I shot it.
Right here. Through the head.

You must know the mountains I mean, now.

Variations on the Theme of Love and Death

"The bread is fresh?"

"Oh yes, yes. Every morning."

Jerónimo has many stories. When days are unclouded he relives them as he follows the beach from the bakery back to the house, leaving imprints in the sand whose memory the sea quickly washes away. There are choices for the narrative even here: to walk or stand, to leave behind sharp cuts or rounded depressions like feet kissing earth. Today Jerónimo leaves his shoes on, because the earth has not done much for him lately and he doesn't feel in its debt. There were times, oh, there were times when the earth rolled beneath him like a lover's body and the sea seduced him, turned like bed covers salty with possibility.

Lately, the earth has not done much. Only been there as a sort of leering reminder. Of where he is. A glass bottom marking the boundary of his life.

Crazy López dreamed up so many schemes. The glass-bottomed boat, for example. Not long ago, but Jerónimo can hardly believe he is still alive to remember it; thinking tourists would come to this dying town, washed up on this littered South American shore with about as many admirers as an aging poet.

The memory infuriates Jerónimo anew as he heads toward his house on the beach: there was peace, all clear and shining like a universe worn out and finally allowing itself sleep.

"Look, friend, that's the catch. Nobody's expecting tourists and we'll have the jump on them all, don't 'cha see?'

Jerónimo had been Crazy's only customer, they knelt and waited hours for a school of tiny silver fish to dart by like a lightning strike at a distance. Only down in the water, it looked so peaceful.

The memory infuriates Jerónimo anew as he heads toward his house on the beach: there was peace, all clear and shining like a universe worn out and finally allowing itself sleep. And there they were, the two idiots, peering down at it. Without a chance of becoming part of that world. He needs to breathe. In any case, he can hardly swim, and the cataracts mean he's as good as blind without his glasses. *That glass bottom became a ceiling,* thinks Jerónimo. *I am an insect under an inverted glass, bumping against the walls.*

Just like years ago in Paris they bumped the railings as they descended the stairs from the hotel, heady with wrongdoing. Her red hair still damp from their bath in the black tub, sprayed tiny drops as she shook her head because she couldn't believe what they had just done. But she laughed a little, too, and even displaced in time her laughter relaxes him now as he heads toward home. Because even if she never belonged to him, she didn't belong to his son either, after that. And perhaps that's all he set out to prove, he tells himself, ignoring the depth of her eyes which is what he drowned in, initially. He never felt at all guilty. They were both men. That had nothing to do with them being father and son, only with them both wanting the same woman; *her brown eyes.*

There is a lilt now in Jerónimo's walk along the beach as he remembers her embrace, her kiss; not the anger that came later or her final words, destined to be repeated many times by countless women: "Get out of my house. Just get out." Nobody around now to tell him to get out of his house, his elegant little hovel huddled by the water. Today Jerónimo leaves his shoes on; today he walks the sand woundingly. He wants to leave his mark, he has no desire to fit into this drunken sorry little town. It's not like the old days –

Which in some cases, were downright awful, Jerónimo snorts suddenly with laughter, does an "I've seen worse times" dance, stomping on the beach near the Hovel. Sorry, the Poet's Estate. Neruda had Isla Negra, he has this. Jerónimo chortles to himself, clutching his morning bread. He notices as he leans over that his zipper has opened. Once that would've caused a stir, with his girlfriend or young wife, with the spouse of one of his sons. Now? He can wander all over this rag of a town and nobody will notice. Maybe a child will chirp, "Lookit señor, zipper's falling," and clasp her hands over her mouth. Ah, what's the use? thinks Jerónimo. Let the thing stay open. Let his old sausage hang out if it feels like it, nobody's interested in an old man's sausage except the old man.

Yeah, the old days. He had dropped out of the university and his family never wanted to see him again, so long as he kept up the binges; sick and unconscious on the front steps one too many times. His siblings – one sister and two brothers, *was it?* After finding out that the woman he called mother was actually the housekeeper, Jerónimo had some doubts about all his relatives.

*Today Jerónimo leaves his shoes on; today
he walks the road woundingly. He wants to
leave the mark, be true to his form, to fit into
this*

Jerónimo gets home and swings open the front door, makes a
grand entrance and imagines introducing himself to the
brothers and sister he remembers mainly as children. "Yes,
hello, I am the family embarrassment, also Poet and
Outstanding Literary Figure. How d'you do?" Takes a little
bow. Jerónimo puts the bread down on the table, uncorks the
bottle of Gato Blanco and pours himself the first one of the
day, not counting the bit of red he had to drain from his
toothbrush glass that morning before using it. So what about
his family. There were always the prostitutes; they'd been
very kind to him.

Very kind, in the beat-up brothel that lay against the soggy
hills of that part of the country, where moisture condensed
and ran in rivulets down the walls. The nights that had been
so cold, the mattresses that sagged in the middle with your
weight like a sack of potatoes in a hammock. Hotel "Wings
of the Angel": a grand place for a boy whose life was lost and
the loss of no concern. If one of the women found him
unconscious in the plaza, or vomiting at the pier, they
dragged him to the brothel and left him lying face down on
the floor of his room. It was good of them, the company at
nights and the occasional meal when he didn't surface for a
few days. More than once he woke up to a throb on the door
like kicks to the head. To Nora or Valentina or one of the
other women, yelling, "Hey poet, you dead? You want some
soup, poet?" Jerónimo is hunting through the drawer for a
knife, to cut the bread. What they didn't know, though, what
those women didn't know was that the pier was his favourite
place to vomit. Do you know why? Because the fish had
come in droves, like fireworks contracting. It didn't matter to
them whose stomach the food had been in, just like it made
little difference to the women, who entered their bodies at
night.

Jerónimo figures maybe he'll work on a collage today. He's done many of them, been at it for years. His favourite shape is a fluid figure eight. It reminds him of the infinite possibilities of each little bit, of every one of the hundreds that make up each collage. He has arranged tributes to great artists out of photographs of their work. Jerónimo bites into a hunk of bread, pours another drink and raises his tumbler. *To my fellow insects.*

In the days when he could really drink, the table would've been surrounded by friends. And not here, in this whistle-stop for nobody before falling off the edge of a continent. It would've been in Paris, or Hamburg, or Bucharest, where so many had gone after the military coup. Bucharest had more Chileans at one time, more Chileans than this town has probably, Jerónimo thinks. He should really do some work. This is what he always wanted: to be left alone to work. Now he's certainly been left alone. Of course, he always figured he'd be left with a little more money, without cataracts, in a house, just a good little house somewhere. Not in the butt-end of the universe.

Jerónimo considers his half-finished collage, number twelve in the *Illuminations* sequence. The bottom of the page is dominated by images of saints, halos fractured but discernible behind their lit heads, eyes turned upward in worship. Many pairs of eyes turned upward. At the top of the page are the dirtiest sex scenes he could cut from his collection of pornographic magazines. Yawning orifices, vulvas red and parted by fingers to show the entryway to a glistening vagina. Many erect penises, some entering the lipsticked mouths of women. *Heh heh. Here's your Immaculate Conception*, thinks Jerónimo. *Here's your standard illumination, the saints' eyes turned up in yearning, awe and fear.*

Yeah, I'm a clever old man.

The sacred and the profane. Pretty clever, all this, Jerónimo sighs as he brushes away some bread crumbs from his chest. Bet he's the first one ever to have thought of it. Jerónimo turns away from the collage, disgusted, to look out the window. He doesn't want to work on that stupid idea. All his grand plans. Some artist. When did he last write? he asks himself. What has he been working with? Old porn magazines and newspapers. When he wanted more dimension, he started pasting his little chewed-off images around empty toilet paper rolls. *There's a statement on art.* Jerónimo poses the question, what do you suppose they'll do with his cupboard full of fancy toilet rolls after he's gone? Mount them on polished wood platforms, cover them with miniature glass domes to ward off dust and deterioration? *Genius, simply genius.*

Once upon a time in the vendor's market in Santiago, Jerónimo had displayed some of his books, cloudy plastic covering the jackets. They were all old, since publishers hadn't wanted anything of his in years – soon after he finished the story of Michaela, the circus flea, the cataracts got in the way of the typewriter keys and he could never touch-type. And among his books on display, Jerónimo put out one or two flat collages, took out a magazine and began another one, tiny figure eight by figure eight, with white glue in a plastic bottle beside him. And a boy, a kid maybe eleven years old, riveted his eyes on him from across the way. *An artist*, thought Jerónimo. And Jerónimo considered the tragedy of this kid, this rag, this seller of potatoes. Thought maybe he'd write about this boy whose heart wanted to create, to make something grow from his mind and soul rather than from the thin dirt. The boy watched for hours. Jerónimo thought he would approach him afterwards, maybe offer him one of his smaller pieces. Gestures like that can change a life. But it was the kid who finally approached him, who finally said, dirt on his face and a wooden splinter thoughtfully chewed on: "Eh, you don't look like an idiot to me. So. How come you're stickin' bits of paper like a baby? Bin watchin ya and you've bin at it for hours, just stickin' bits of paper."

Feeling the kid's breath still fresh in his ear Jerónimo is surprised to find himself sprawled on his kitchen table. He has almost fallen asleep, his glasses have slipped off and everything is cloudy, like swimming through milk. He has spilled wine on the collage, the twelfth in the *Illuminations* sequence. Jerónimo retrieves his glasses and decides he doesn't care about the collage. *They're all the same, the other eleven will do just fine since nobody will look at them. Maybe some dirty old guy who'll wish the rest of the pictures were there. Who'll think it's a flaw that they're rearranged.* Jerónimo pours more wine, sops up the spill with his shirt. Thinks if Fresia were there she would bring him another shirt. Fresia was the last one, the last one to make the same request and finally mean it. That he had to get out. That he was making them all crazy, her and the girls. "Like a big old baby," she said in a tone more sad than angry.

Fresia never understood. She had wanted him to fix the roof, to pay for the gas. She never understood that when Jerónimo stood looking out the window, as he often did for hours, that was hard work. If she stood at the window, she wouldn't think the things that he did. That's why she cooked and paid the bills. His youngest, Gabriela, she knew her old man. A little thing with wispy hair, but tough as nails. A few years ago she had presented him with her first collection of poetry, *Laughter of Lilies*. Not bad, for a first try. Jerónimo expected that Fresia's greying black hair would fall over her face, messed and tear-dampened, when he died. Even though she was the one who had told him to get out. But his tough girl, Gaby, she would go to his grave, and read to him, perhaps. She would leave flowers and poems strewn over the fresh soil.

Now his first book, that was a wild story. Jerónimo realizes he has only picked at the bread a bit, but the bottle is empty. He rummages in the pantry suspecting he might have another bottle in there, and sure enough there's one at the back. Jerónimo uncorks it with considerable effort and pours himself a tumbler, using the opportunity to spill a little more on the last piece in the *Illuminations* sequence, which he has decided he hates. As much as he did that first book. *Yeah, those were some days – the days of the brothel, of his first book. Things that can change a life.*

Like regaining consciousness one day to Nora hammering her fists on the other side of the door, not asking if he was dead but saying: "Open up, I'm serious. He's downstairs for real, NE-RU-DA. Can you hear me, poet? I'm not kidding. Says you wrote to him – oh!" which was out of surprise. Because Neruda himself had gotten a key from the madam and was ushering Nora out of the way so he could open the door. Jerónimo sat on the floor, convinced he was hallucinating. And Neruda, this man of words so beautiful they hurt, walked in and threw Jerónimo's dirty underwear from the only chair in the room, sat and made small talk before getting to the point: "Very impressed with the work you sent. I think I can get my publisher to do a book for you, if you can produce more of this. "

Neruda accompanied the delivery men when they brought
Jerónimo the entire first edition of his book, *Variations on
the Theme of Love and Death*. Small, square, very well
bound. Then, sitting on top of the boxes leafing through
it, after Neruda had gone, Jerónimo *thought: nothing but
scribbles, things nobody will read*. In that realization
Jerónimo felt a foreshadowing of the same sinking of the
gut, the crumbling of an interior lining of the body, as he
felt years after that when a kid in a market place asked him,
"How come? You don't look like an idiot to me." So
Jerónimo stood, flinging a copy of the book into the air,
did a "let's have a whing-ding" jig, invited
the prostitutes and his bar buddies over with
much wine and
two or three cans of gasoline.

A little here, a little there, open all the windows so the
smoke won't choke anybody who's not already uncon-
scious. Just one box at a time and luckily the madam was
out, so she didn't see the smoke mushrooming from the
window, where Jerónimo leaned out to reassure passersby.
"Everything's fine. No, no, we're just having a little party.
No, no need. It's well under control." He was very careful
because, after all, they had been good to him at the brothel
and he didn't want to cause any trouble. With wet towels
he and a few of the others contained the fire if it reached
the floor, took turns standing on the only chair in the
room and slapping at the ceiling if it caught even a little.
Best party he ever threw.

Jerónimo didn't regret it for a minute, not even when the
madam stood in her thick high heels among the charred

And then what happened? What happened?
Jerónimo wandered away. There was a woman.
Maybe it was Fresia but he can't say for sure,
he can't see her face because his eyes are
damaged by cataracts.

boxes, books strewn like pieces of burnt toast, and shook her head. It was just a bit too much, she explained, after all she had her home and business to protect, and sorry though she was, Jerónimo would have to leave. The walls bore a grey film, and there was an awful smell Jerónimo couldn't identify. On the bright side, Jerónimo thought, probably a good percentage of the cockroaches were gone to look for alternate living arrangements. Neruda didn't understand, didn't speak to him for fourteen years.

When Neruda took him back, Jerónimo worked as his secretary for a while. But gradually he completed fewer and fewer of his duties and eventually he just lived on Isla Negra, for a time. And then what happened? *What happened?* Jerónimo wandered away. There was a woman. Maybe it was Fresia but he can't say for sure, he can't see her face because his eyes are damaged by cataracts. The government was overthrown amid gunfire on television and Neruda was suddenly dead. Not from gunshots. Not from cancer, or whatever they blamed officially. He died from disappointment.

Jerónimo cries gently now, his white head in his hands, another tumbler of wine spilled and his elbows sitting in its red puddle. Neruda is gone, he has been gone now for almost twenty years, since before Fresia, since before the girls. Almost everyone who was with Jerónimo then, is gone. The few who are left don't return his letters. They used to send him money when he was in a fix, now some of them don't even believe he's going blind, they think it's another one of his stories. And that whole glorious world, seedy as it was with its prostitutes and the magical appearance of poets, is gone. All those women are dead, or huddled in marketplaces, rattling around in dry, old bodies that haven't opened to anybody in years, like his own.

And what has he left behind? His shoeprints, three wives, countless affairs. His five sons, all men now, two of whom he betrayed with their wives. Fresia, who still writes but doesn't invite him to visit, afraid he'll stay. His three girls, Gabriela the youngest like a ramrod, her juvenile poetry brought to him as an offer of understanding. Everyone scattered over several continents. He has left some work, some books. Actually, more than twenty, some of which have been translated and sold in the millions. So what? So millions of people have forgotten him.

This is his crowning moment: not the birth of his first child, or his first love affair, which, actually, he doesn't even remember. It happened when he went to look at a house for rent in Santiago. For himself and Mariela, a beautiful girl, if she would agree to move in with him. After he walked through the house he carefully printed his name on a piece of paper and said he'd be interested, at a lower price. And the owners, a middle-aged couple with a comfortable air of wealth, exchanged a single look after reading his name and the man gushed, "Oh Mr. Cárdenas, we didn't realize who you were. Please, you must take the house, no charge, it costs us nothing to maintain. It would be our privilege to provide you with a setting for your work for the time that you need it. "

His crowning moment: *understanding*.

Jerónimo is crying, his face streaked and red, his nose running onto his sleeve. All he ever wanted was understanding, freedom from the mediocre limits. To escape the glass dome, dive under the surface. Maybe his crowning moment didn't happen exactly that way; after all he's a

great liar. He has so many stories he has trouble remember-
ing which ones are true. Maybe he only burned a couple of
his first books and it's possible that his sons' wives rejected
him, as so many others did. But the house, that was his best
time, real or created. He did live in Santiago rent-free for a
year once. He can't recall the details of how that came about.
Now he has wandered the globe and reached the end of a
continent. The sea that once linked him with the world, now
insists on his limits: you are here, you are here, you are here.
The glass floor. The earth that once turned beneath him like
a lover's body, the ocean that now washes his prints from the
sand and beats each day closer to his door.

If he were to reach the gates of St. Peter, Jerónimo would
show him the *Illuminations* sequence. He would introduce
himself: "Pleased to meet you. I am an old man."

This is how Jerónimo's last story ends: he rises from the
table, slowly, methodically, and stands for some minutes at
the door, listening to the sea. It is one, maybe two in the
afternoon. He shuts the door deliberately and removes his
belt from the loops of his pants. Climbing on the table, he
eases the belt through the buckle and fixes the dangling end
onto the ship hook that hangs from the rafter, which he's had
his eye on for a while. Then, quickly and with a fluid motion
surprising in an old man, he slips his grey head through the
noose and kicks the table out from under him. The earth, in
any case, has not done much for him lately. The wine bottle
explodes against the shelf like a small cherry bomb, the
soaked bread plops to the ground and the final collage in the
Illuminations sequence, unfinished, drifts down in a quick,
graceful swoop.

Poem for Jerónimo

 You marvelled at the dishonesty of others,
because your events slipped
between our fingers, left us
showing our empty palms
and saying, *see? I have nothing.*
That Jerónimo, he's a fabulous liar.
Our eyes offended your sensibilities – we saw only
the obvious, rotting fruit in your shiny seeds,
dirty clothes on your beautiful fishermen.

In a way, Jerónimo, you were already one foot
on the other side, slipping
to intangibility. You slept not in your bed
but sprawled between poems, layered like blankets,
or on a park bench in one
of the countries of the collages
you glued obsessively,
piecing together a more desirable world.
You were fading into light, curling
into smoke from your cigarettes, sifting
into the sand that crept from the beach to your back door.
Already we could reach right through you.

If you can see any further from whatever
height you've found,
quick, Jerónimo, tell me.
There is the moon,
its reflection in the ocean
and the ocean itself.
Which one is most true?

For all that you were a tough old bastard, you were just
too delicate to hang on to – you came undone in our hands
like fish nets crumbling to dust. When you died,
you did it so that each of us would know
we'd been there, hoisting
the end of your rope.

We didn't lie to you, Jerónimo. We didn't
pack like wolves behind your back to gnaw
through everything that you held evident.

If you can see any further from whatever
height you've found,
quick, Jerónimo, tell me.
There is the moon,
its reflection in the ocean
and the ocean itself.
Which one is most true?

Other titles available from Insomniac Press:

Portfolio One
by Mike O'Connor, David Blackmore, & Monica Dobrov
This first collection of chapbooks represents the blending of media: the prose & poetry become design elements as the written word defines and inspires the design. In *Dream Home*, a collection of poems and a short story by Mike O'Connor, the focus is on people and images that survive in the gaps created by society. *The Silence Inbetween* examines the artificiality of life and the inevitability of love through poetry and prose by David Blackmore. *Tourist Season*, three short stories set in Cuba written and designed by Monica Dobrov, examine conflicting points of view from several diverse characters. All chapbooks are accordion-folded and contained within a limited edition, hand-painted fabric pocket.
6 1/2" x 6" chapbooks, $9.99

Portfolio Two
by Zaffi Gousopoulos, Paula Gillis, Marni Norwich and Mike O'Connor
The second collection of chapbooks incorporates quarter-folded chapbooks within a custom-made fine paper folder. *The Playing Field* contains poetry and prose by Zaffi Gousopoulos. It mythologizes the evolution of the author as a writer in a light-hearted and satirical style. *Pool* is a short story adaptation of a dramatic monologue by Paula Gillis. Gillis details her discovery and love of the best game in the world: pool. Two short stories by Marni Norwich show differing glimpses into the rites of passage into womanhood in *Point of Kiss*. Mike O'Connor continues his exploration of shadows and darkness in *Writing on the Edge of a Shadow*. It is at times a fantastic, grotesque and comic collection of poetry and prose.
6" x 9 1/2" chapbooks, $12.99

Mad Angels and Amphetamines
by Nik Beat, Noah Leznoff, Mary Elizabeth Grace and Matthew Remski
A collection by four emerging Canadian writers and three graphic designers. In this book, design is an integral part of the prose and poetry. Each writer collaborated with a designer so that the graphic design is an interpretation of the writer's works. Nik Beat's lyrical and unpretentious poetry; Noah Leznoff's dark humour prose and narrative poetic cycles; Mary Elizabeth Grace's Celtic dialogues and mystical images; and Matthew Remski's medieval symbols and surrealistic style of story; this is the mixture of styles that weave together in *Mad Angels and Amphetamines*.
6" x 9" trade paperback, $12.95

For information about this press or to order any of these titles, please send a cheque or money order (include $1.50 for shipping and taxes) to:
Insomniac Press, 378 Delaware Avenue, Toronto, Canada, M6H 2T8